Dark TEMPTATIONS

Annie Jocoby

VINCI
BOOKS

By Annie Jocoby

Temptations

Vinci Books

vinci-books.com

Published by Vinci Books Ltd in 2026

1

The publisher and the author have made every effort to obtain permissions
for any third party material used in this book and to comply with copyright
law. Any queries in this respect should be brought to the attention of the
publisher and any omissions will be corrected in future editions.

A CIP catalogue record for this book is available from the British Library.

Paperback ISBN: 9781036703134

The EU GPSR authorised representative is Logos Europe, 9 rue Nicolas
Poussion, 17000 La Rochelle, France contact@logoseurope.eu

Chapter One

Serena

I continued to look out the window, watching for Slade. I had to get out of here, but Derek was sitting on his porch, looking over at my house. I didn't know if he was doing that to intimidate me, but if that was the reason, he was succeeding.

Come on, Serena. You're braver than this. He's only a man. A man who managed to ruin my life, to be sure, but still only a man. What was he going to do? What could he do to me that he hadn't already done?

He was still violent, though. I knew that from meeting his girlfriend. Maggie was covering up as best she could, but I knew her secret. Since I knew that Derek was still violent, I really needed to make sure that I avoided him as much as I could.

Slade finally arrived, and came straight into the house. I wrapped my arms around him and held him ever so tightly. I wanted to just feel him, and know that with his arms

ANNIE JOCOBY

around me, I felt truly safe. He would take care of that jackass next door if I needed him to. I knew this.

"What's going on Serena?" he asked me finally, after I had held onto him for what seemed like an eternity.

"My new next door neighbor. It's him. Derek. The man who has haunted me my entire life. He's living right next door."

He looked at me with understanding, and I could tell that he had suspected that this was going to happen. "I'm not surprised. Charlotte is getting her revenge. She can't kill you, but she can certainly make your life a living hell."

"I think that I need to leave for awhile. Can I stay with you?"

"Of course, I was hoping you would say that." He hesitated. "But Serena, I have a feeling that you're not going be able to totally get away from him."

"What does that mean?"

He took a deep breath. "Charlotte and I have some understandings, and it's very delicate right now. I don't know if I can trust her. I have these blackmail documents, so she's restrained somewhat. But one false move and you could very well find yourself in grave danger."

I didn't like the way he was talking, but I had to let him finish. "Okay. Go ahead and tell me what's going on."

"One of the stipulations that Charlotte made was that your firm would have to be the one to represent my mother in her murder trial, assuming that there is a murder trial, of course."

I narrowed my eyes. "Okay. That doesn't seem so bad so far."

Then it hit me. Maggie told me that Derek had a very lucrative offer with a law firm in town. I suddenly knew exactly which firm he was going to work for.

Slade confirmed my suspicions. "I have a feeling that Derek is going to be working at your firm."

I felt my heart drop to my knees. "Okay. Well then, I'll just have to find another job." I hated that I still felt that I couldn't be around him. I felt like a total coward, just cutting and running, but I couldn't have him around. My psyche felt fragile all of a sudden, as what had happened to me in those woods so long ago came flooding back. I felt like it was yesterday in a lot of ways. It was certainly still haunting me as if it were yesterday.

He nodded his head. "Yes, you will have to find another job. But my mother has to be represented by your firm."

"Well, that's impossible. I want to represent her. I need to represent her. I can do an awesome job on her case. I've tried cases like hers before, and I can be very persuasive with a jury."

"I know all that. But Charlotte's stipulation for agreeing not to harm you is that only your firm can represent mom. As I said, I think that she's full of crap, but I would prefer not to find that out for sure, if you know what I mean."

I was faced with another decision. I could cut and run and let Margot be represented by another attorney on the firm. Any other attorney wasn't going to be as passionate as I was about giving Margot excellent representation. Her case was going to be precarious anyhow. If I let another attorney try her case, there was a very good chance that he or she would lose. And Slade's mother would spend the rest of her life in prison.

Or, I could stick around the firm. I would have to see Derek every single day, assuming that Slade was correct in saying that Charlotte made sure that Derek had a job at my firm.

"You've put me in an untenable position," I said, stating

3

the brutally obvious. Then I shook my head. "Sorry, that was uncalled for. Charlotte is the one who has put me in an untenable position." I tried not to think about the possibility that my first statement was correct – that Slade had put me in this position. He was the one who brought the poison known as Charlotte into my world. His actions were the ones that gave her so much power to begin with, starting with that night when he decided to cover up what his mother did.

Slade said nothing, but just wrapped his arms around me tightly. I tried to feel comforted by his touch and his scent, but I couldn't. All I could think about was the fact that I was going to be subjected to Derek. Even if I cut and run and moved in with Slade permanently – that wasn't quite on the table, although I had no doubt he would ask me to do so if that was what I wanted – I could never get away from Derek at all. He would be at my workplace every single day, and I couldn't just quit and leave Margot high and dry like that.

I suddenly felt sick. "Well, what's done is done. I need to leave this house." I had packed a bag of things, and my work clothes were in hanger bags. Bella and Gigi were in their traveling kennels. I was ready to go. "Let's get out of here."

As we left, we noticed that Derek was sitting on his porch swing, drinking a beer. He leered at me as Slade and I left, his beer to his lips, which were curled in a derisive smile.

Slade packed my things in the car, and asked me to wait for him in the front seat. I then looked out the window and saw him standing on Derek's porch, his hands on his hips. He seemed to be intently speaking with, who was looking angrier and angrier. At one point, Derek stood from his seat on the swing, and Slade pushed him back down. Derek immediately got back up, his fists balled up tight. He swung at Slade, who ducked and landed an uppercut fist right in Derek's stomach. Derek doubled over in pain, but rapidly got back up and punched Slade's face.

It was soon full on, as the two men scuffled on the porch for what seemed to be an eternity. I was almost in awe of Slade's cat-like grace that showed itself when he fought. He was in amazing shape, and he rapidly danced around Derek like a prize-fighter. He wasn't just a street pugilist, randomly throwing punches and hoping that they landed. He was more strategic than that, and showed a great deal of finesse. The upshot was that he landed many more punches on Derek than Derek did on him, and finally, he stood victorious over Derek, who was crumpled up on the porch.

Slade finally came to the car, after it looked like he had thoroughly lectured a crumpled Derek. "Let's go," he said.

"What was that all about?"

"Nothing."

I got quiet. I didn't like Slade not talking to me about the scuffle on the porch. At the same time, I knew that Slade was infuriated, and he just needed to calm down a little bit. He would talk to me when he was good and ready.

I watched him as his tense hands gripped the wheel. He stared straight ahead at the road, not saying a single word. His jaw was clenched tightly, and he kept shaking his head. "Bastard," he mumbled under his breath a few times.

I put my hand on his leg. "I hate to tell you this, but you're doing 90," I told him as he raced down the highway. He was passing everyone on the road, which was saying something, considering drivers routinely went 80 MPH or above on this highway.

He still said nothing as he weaved in and out of cars.

I sighed, looking out the window as the world passed by me at a faster-than-usual rate. I had no idea what to expect when I got to his house. I knew that Margot was there, but I didn't think that she was aware of what fate awaited her.

"I hate that bastard, and I hate that he wants to intimidate you," Slade finally said. "I told him that he was going to leave you alone at the workplace."

I nodded my head. "I can fight my own battles," I said weakly. Ordinarily, that was completely true. I had always been independent and a fighter. But with this situation…I didn't know if I could fight this battle. Derek had taken so much from me at such a young age. What he had done shaped me, and not necessarily for the better.

Slade put his arm around my neck as he continued to steer the car on the highway. "Serena, you can't handle this on your own. I know that you want to, but trust me, you need somebody in your corner on this. I know how to handle slimy assholes like Derek."

I tried to tamp down a little smile that was threatening. Truth be told, I liked to see this part of him. This protective instinct that he had for me was something that was almost intoxicating. "How do you handle him, other than giving him a beat-down? And, by the way, you're still technically out on bail. I anticipate that the prosecutors are going to drop the charges against you as soon as that video is authenticated, but that's still not a 100% guarantee. I would suggest you keeping your temper in check for the time being."

He sighed. "You find your opponent's weakness and exploit it. That's the only way to handle difficult people. With Charlotte, I blackmail her. With this guy, I threaten. He's a typical bully-coward, which means that he's easily intimidated. He'll never admit to being intimidated, because he's all about surface bluster. But, deep down, he can be intimidated by somebody who actually stands up to him. Or should I say he can be intimidated by a man who stands up to him. He'll still run over any woman, because he sees them as being weaker than he is. He won't run over me. Trust me on this."

"What did you threaten him with?"

He shrugged. "I just told him that I knew who he was and what he did, and he needed to watch his ass. If I heard anything from you about him treating you disrespectfully, I would expose him for who he is. I saw fear in his eyes when I was saying those things to him."

"Why don't you expose him? Or, for that matter, I can expose him."

Slade gave me the side-eye. "Two reasons. One, you don't have proof of anything. Two, him working with you was one of Charlotte's stipulations for not harming you. I have to work through what's going on with her. I need to test her a little, see how much she's bluffing and how dead serious she is about putting you in danger at her whim. I can't just do things willy-nilly that are going to piss her off, at least not until I figure out her game just a little better."

"She has her pound of flesh with your mother and with you for that matter. I would imagine that you're also going to be in quite a lot of trouble once the prosecutor finds out that you helped your mother dump that body. And you do know that I cannot represent both of you, because that would be a conflict of interest." It was always difficult to represent co-conspirators, as there was always the chance that one would be offered a deal to roll on the other. I didn't necessarily think that would be the case here, but if there was that possibility, I couldn't represent them both.

Slade shrugged his shoulders. "I have a very high-powered attorney on retainer in LA. I'm not concerned for myself." He took a deep breath. "Are you up to this? Defending my mother? She wants to speak with you tonight about her options. I want you to give it to her clearly and without bullshit. She needs to know what she's up against."

Out of the frying pan, into the fire. "I think that you know what she's up against. Hugh's blood is at her old apartment, and, with Charlotte's tip, I have no doubt your mother will be charged in his murder. She was out on parole for another murder at the time she killed Hugh. It's going to be an uphill battle for sure. I can get an expert witness who specializes in post-traumatic stress disorder to testify that your mother was reasonable in feeling threatened by Hugh at the time that she killed him. If the jury can buy that she was reasonable in feeling that Hugh was going to rape her, we can win a self-defense argument. If the jury isn't persuaded that her actions were reasonable, she'll go to prison for murder. It's all going to hinge on what I can convince the jury to believe about how threatened she felt, and whether or not a reasonable person in her shoes would feel the same."

Slade nodded. "I actually do know all of that, but I wanted her to hear all that from you. She has to have the confidence that you can represent her zealously, and you won't let a single stone go unturned. I'm counting on you."

Suddenly, I felt pressured. More pressured than I had ever felt at any time in my life. "Slade," I said, feeling nauseated. "You have to understand that the odds are against us here. Even under the best readings of the facts, your mother shouldn't have done what she did. I don't blame her for getting a gun and wanting to defend herself but she probably should have just told him to leave. I would imagine he would have just left, as it was a choice between getting out of there alive or getting shot. She shot him, no questions asked. It's not going to be easy to get her off of this."

Slade was staring straight ahead. We had arrived at his home, and he was just staring out the windshield of his car. I wasn't sure if he had heard me when I was talking to him, so I touched him on the shoulder. He jumped a little when my hand landed on his body. He shook his head. "I know that the odds are against my mother," he finally said after a long pause. "Believe me, I understand that. I'm relying on you to beat the odds."

"I'm hoping I can, too. But Slade, I don't want it to come between us if something happens. I feel that you're going to always blame me."

All at once, Slade looked angry. Really angry. "What are you saying? Are you telling me that you don't want to represent my mother? If that's what you're saying, then just say it. I'll find another attorney at your firm to represent her. I'm sure that there are plenty of lawyers at your firm that will jump at the chance to seize my healthy retainer for mom's representation."

"Slade. No. Calm down. I'm just expressing my concern that things between you and I might change if I lose this case. That's all."

He narrowed his eyes. "Then don't lose."

At that, he got out of the car and walked towards the house. I reluctantly followed him, feeling as if I was a prisoner who was being led to the death chamber. I walked slowly and deliberately, trying to slow down the process. I didn't want to face Margot and tell her the truth. I didn't want to see those eyes. She was going to look at me with hope, and, by the time I got through telling her what I needed to tell her about her chances, she was going to be in tears. The hope would be drained from her eyes. I had seen that particular transformation too many times in my position.

The last thing I wanted was to see that transformation happen in Margot's eyes.

Even so, I knew I was about to see just that.

Chapter Two

I continued to look out the window, watching for Slade. I had to get out of here, but Derek was sitting on his porch, looking over at my house. I didn't know if he was doing that to intimidate me, but if that was the reason, he was succeeding.

Come on, Serena. You're braver than this. He's only a man. A man who managed to ruin my life, to be sure, but still only a man. What was he going to do? What could he do to me that he hadn't already done?

He was still violent, though. I knew that from meeting his girlfriend. Maggie was covering up as best she could, but I knew her secret. Since I knew that Derek was still violent, I really needed to make sure that I avoided him as much as I could.

Slade finally arrived, and came straight into the house. I wrapped my arms around him and held him ever so tightly. I wanted to just feel him, and know that with his arms around me, I felt truly safe. He would take care of that jackass next door if I needed him to. I knew this.

"What's going on Serena?" he asked me finally, after I had held onto him for what seemed like an eternity.

"My new next door neighbor. It's him. Derek. The man who has haunted me my entire life. He's living right next door."

He looked at me with understanding, and I could tell that he had suspected that this was going to happen. "I'm not surprised. Charlotte is getting her revenge. She can't kill you, but she can certainly make your life a living hell."

"I think that I need to leave for awhile. Can I stay with you?"

"Of course, I was hoping you would say that." He hesitated. "But Serena, I have a feeling that you're not going be able to totally get away from him."

"What does that mean?"

He took a deep breath. "Charlotte and I have some understandings, and it's very delicate right now. I don't know if I can trust her. I have these blackmail documents, so she's restrained somewhat. But one false move and you could very well find yourself in grave danger."

I didn't like the way he was talking, but I had to let him finish. "Okay. Go ahead and tell me what's going on."

"One of the stipulations that Charlotte made was that your firm would have to be the one to represent my mother in her murder trial, assuming that there is a murder trial, of course."

I narrowed my eyes. "Okay. That doesn't seem so bad so far."

Then it hit me. Maggie told me that Derek had a very lucrative offer with a law firm in town. I suddenly knew exactly which firm he was going to work for.

Slade confirmed my suspicions. "I have a feeling that Derek is going to be working at your firm."

I felt my heart drop to my knees. "Okay. Well then, I'll just have to find another job." I hated that I still felt that I couldn't be around him. I felt like a total coward, just cutting and running, but I couldn't have him around. My psyche felt fragile all of a sudden, as what had happened to me in those woods so long ago came flooding back. I felt like it was yesterday in a lot of ways. It was certainly still haunting me as if it were yesterday.

He nodded his head. "Yes, you will have to find another job. But my mother has to be represented by your firm."

"Well, that's impossible. I want to represent her. I need to represent her. I can do an awesome job on her case. I've tried cases like hers before, and I can be very persuasive with a jury."

"I know all that. But Charlotte's stipulation for agreeing not to harm you is that only your firm can represent mom. As I said, I think that she's full of crap, but I would prefer not to find that out for sure, if you know what I mean."

I was faced with another decision. I could cut and run and let Margot be represented by another attorney on the firm. Any other attorney wasn't going to be as passionate as I was about giving Margot excellent representation. Her case was going to be precarious anyhow. If I let another attorney try her case, there was a very good chance that he or she would lose. And Slade's mother would spend the rest of her life in prison.

Or, I could stick around the firm. I would have to see Derek every single day, assuming that Slade was correct in saying that Charlotte made sure that Derek had a job at my firm.

"You've put me in an untenable position," I said, stating the brutally obvious. Then I shook my head. "Sorry, that was uncalled for. Charlotte is the one who has put me in an untenable position." I tried not to think about the possibility that my first statement was correct – that Slade had put me in this position. He was the one who brought the poison known as Charlotte into my world. His actions were the ones that gave her so much power to begin with, starting with that night when he decided to cover up what his mother did.

Slade said nothing, but just wrapped his arms around me tightly. I tried to feel comforted by his touch and his scent, but I couldn't. All I could think about was the fact that I was going to be subjected to Derek. Even if I cut and run and moved in with Slade permanently – that wasn't quite on the table, although I had no doubt he would ask me to do so if that was what I wanted – I could never get away from Derek at all. He would be at my workplace every single day, and I couldn't just quit and leave Margot high and dry like that.

I suddenly felt sick. "Well, what's done is done. I need to leave this house." I had packed a bag of things, and my work clothes were in hanger bags. Bella and Gigi were in their traveling kennels. I was ready to go. "Let's get out of here."

As we left, we noticed that Derek was sitting on his porch swing, drinking a beer. He leered at me as Slade and I left, his beer to his lips, which were curled in a derisive smile.

Slade packed my things in the car, and asked me to wait for him in the front seat. I then looked out the window and saw him standing on Derek's porch, his hands on his hips. He seemed to be intently speaking with, who was looking angrier and angrier. At one point, Derek stood from his seat on the swing, and Slade pushed him back down. Derek immediately got back up, his fists balled up tight. He swung at Slade, who ducked and landed an uppercut fist right in Derek's stomach. Derek doubled over in pain, but rapidly got back up and punched Slade's face.

It was soon full on, as the two men scuffled on the porch for what seemed to be an eternity. I was almost in awe of Slade's cat-like grace that showed itself when he fought. He was in amazing shape, and he rapidly danced around Derek like a prize-fighter. He wasn't just a street pugilist, randomly throwing punches and hoping that they landed. He was more strategic than that, and showed a great deal of finesse. The upshot was that he landed many more punches on Derek than Derek did on him, and finally, he stood victorious over Derek, who was crumpled up on the porch.

Slade finally came to the car, after it looked like he had thoroughly lectured a crumpled Derek. "Let's go," he said.

"What was that all about?"

"Nothing."

I got quiet. I didn't like Slade not talking to me about the scuffle on the porch. At the same time, I knew that Slade was infuriated, and he just needed to calm down a little bit. He would talk to me when he was good and ready.

I watched him as his tense hands gripped the wheel. He stared straight ahead at the road, not saying a single word. His jaw was clenched tightly, and he kept shaking his head. "Bastard," he mumbled under his breath a few times.

I put my hand on his leg. "I hate to tell you this, but you're doing 90," I told him as he raced down the highway. He was passing everyone on the road, which was saying something, considering drivers routinely went 80 MPH or above on this highway.

He still said nothing as he weaved in and out of cars.

I sighed, looking out the window as the world passed by me at a faster-than-usual rate. I had no idea what to expect when I got to his house. I knew that Margot was there, but I didn't think that she was aware of what fate awaited her.

"I hate that bastard, and I hate that he wants to intimidate you," Slade finally said. "I told him that he was going to leave you alone at the workplace."

I nodded my head. "I can fight my own battles," I said weakly. Ordinarily, that was completely true. I had always been independent and a fighter. But with this situation...I didn't know if I could fight this battle. Derek had taken so much from me at such a young age. What he had done shaped me, and not necessarily for the better.

Slade put his arm around my neck as he continued to steer the car on the highway. "Serena, you can't handle this on your own. I know that you want to, but trust me, you need somebody in your corner on this. I know how to handle slimy assholes like Derek."

I tried to tamp down a little smile that was threatening. Truth be told, I liked to see this part of him. This protective instinct that he had for me was something that was almost intoxicating. "How do you handle him, other than giving him a beat-down? And, by the way, you're still technically out on bail. I anticipate that the prosecutors are going to drop the charges against you as soon as that video is authenticated, but that's still not a 100% guarantee. I would suggest you keeping your temper in check for the time being."

He sighed. "You find your opponent's weakness and exploit it. That's the only way to handle difficult people. With Charlotte, I blackmail her. With this guy, I threaten. He's a typical bully-coward, which means that he's easily intimidated. He'll never admit to being intimidated, because he's all about surface bluster. But, deep down, he can be intimidated by somebody who actually stands up to him. Or should I say he can be intimidated by a man who stands up to him. He'll still run over any woman, because he sees them as being weaker than he is. He won't run over me. Trust me on this."

"What did you threaten him with?"

He shrugged. "I just told him that I knew who he was and what he did, and he needed to watch his ass. If I heard anything from you about him treating you disrespectfully, I would expose him for who he is. I saw fear in his eyes when I was saying those things to him."

"Why don't you expose him? Or, for that matter, I can expose him."

Slade gave me the side-eye. "Two reasons. One, you don't have proof of anything. Two, him working with you was one of Charlotte's stipulations for not harming you. I have to work through what's going on with her. I need to test her a little, see how much she's bluffing and how dead serious she is about putting you in danger at her whim. I can't just do things willy-nilly that are going to piss her off, at least not until I figure out her game just a little better."

"She has her pound of flesh with your mother and with you for that matter. I would imagine that you're also going to be in quite a lot of trouble once the prosecutor finds out that you helped your mother dump that body. And you do know that I cannot represent both of you, because that would be a conflict of interest." It was always difficult to represent co-conspirators, as there was always the chance that one would be offered a deal to roll on the other. I didn't necessarily think that would be the case here, but if there was that possibility, I couldn't represent them both.

Slade shrugged his shoulders. "I have a very high-powered attorney on retainer in LA. I'm not concerned for myself." He took a deep breath. "Are you up to this? Defending my mother? She wants to speak with you tonight about her options. I want you to give it to her clearly and without bullshit. She needs to know what she's up against."

Out of the frying pan, into the fire. "I think that you know what she's up against. Hugh's blood is at her old apartment, and, with Charlotte's tip, I have no doubt your mother will be charged in his murder. She was out on parole for another murder at the time she killed Hugh. It's going to be an uphill battle for sure. I can get an expert witness who specializes in post-traumatic stress disorder to testify that your mother was reasonable in feeling threatened by Hugh at the time that she killed him. If the jury can buy that she was reasonable in feeling that Hugh was going to rape her, we can win a self-defense argument. If the jury isn't persuaded that her actions were reasonable, she'll go to prison for murder. It's all going to hinge on what I can convince the jury to believe about how threatened she felt, and whether or not a reasonable person in her shoes would feel the same."

Slade nodded. "I actually do know all of that, but I wanted her to hear all that from you. She has to have the confidence that you can represent her zealously, and you won't let a single stone go unturned. I'm counting on you."

Suddenly, I felt pressured. More pressured than I had ever felt at any time in my life. "Slade," I said, feeling nauseated. "You have to understand that the odds are against us here. Even under the best readings of the facts, your mother shouldn't have done what she did. I don't blame her for getting a gun and wanting to defend herself but she probably should have just told him to leave. I would imagine he would have just left, as it was a choice between getting out of there alive or getting shot. She shot him, no questions asked. It's not going to be easy to get her off of this."

Slade was staring straight ahead. We had arrived at his home, and he was just staring out the windshield of his car. I wasn't sure if he had heard me when I was talking to him, so I touched him on the shoulder. He jumped a little when my hand landed on his body. He shook his head. "I know that the odds are against my mother," he finally said after a long pause. "Believe me, I understand that. I'm relying on you to beat the odds."

"I'm hoping I can, too. But Slade, I don't want it to come between us if something happens. I feel that you're going to always blame me."

All at once, Slade looked angry. Really angry. "What are you saying? Are you telling me that you don't want to represent my mother? If that's what you're saying, then just say it. I'll find another attorney at your firm to represent her. I'm sure that there are plenty of lawyers at your firm that will jump at the chance to seize my healthy retainer for mom's representation."

"Slade. No. Calm down. I'm just expressing my concern that things between you and I might change if I lose this case. That's all."

He narrowed his eyes. "Then don't lose."

At that, he got out of the car and walked towards the house. I reluctantly followed him, feeling as if I was a prisoner who was being led to the death chamber. I walked slowly and deliberately, trying to slow down the process. I didn't want to face Margot and tell her the truth. I didn't want to see those eyes. She was going to look at me with hope, and, by the time I got through telling her what I needed to tell her about her chances, she was going to be in tears. The hope would be drained from her eyes. I had seen that particular transformation too many times in my position.

The last thing I wanted was to see that transformation happen in Margot's eyes.

Even so, I knew I was about to see just that.

20

Chapter Three

The next day, I knew that I had to face what was happening at my work. I wanted to see if Derek was really going to be there when I got there, and then I would have to figure out how to handle his presence. My plan was to ignore him, of course. It was a large enough firm that I really shouldn't have to interact with him, unless he was on one of my teams. I had been informed that as soon as I got my bar results back, assuming I passed, I would have my own legal teams for cases. I would just exclude him from all my teams and pretend he didn't exist.

I shook my head. That sounded like a good plan, but one that probably wouldn't work. Derek was going to be a problem. As much as I wanted him to not be a problem, I knew that he was going to be. Just his presence in the office was going to throw me off my game completely.

I went into the office, and Cindy, who was one of the partners there, greeted me immediately. "Oh my god, Serena, you're here. Sit down. I need to talk to you about some things."

I beckoned her to my office. I didn't like Cindy, nor did I trust her. I had this feeling that she was about to lay some bullshit gossip on me, and I wasn't at all sure that I wanted to hear it. Regardless, by the look on her face, I knew that there was a possibility that her news was serious.

"Sit," I said, gesturing to the chair in front of me. "And I hope you don't mind if I eat this muffin while you talk to me." I had picked up some healthy muffins at a Jamba Juice, and I was preparing to eat one of them.

"Okay," she said, sitting down. "I have some awesome news for you and some terrible news as well."

I simply nodded my head, knowing already what had happened. But I let her speak anyhow. *Try to act surprised, Serena. Do your best acting job.*

She took a deep breath. "Well, I think that you should know the good news first, that way the awful news might not seem so awful."

"Go on."

"Slade's charges are going to be dropped. I just spoke with the prosecutor on the case, and he's calling an emergency hearing next week to formally drop them.. That's great news, isn't it?"

I forced a fake look of surprise on my face and clapped my hands with delight. "That's wonderful news!"

She furrowed her brows. "I thought you would be more excited that this. I mean, he's your boyfriend, isn't he?"

"I can't get excited about anything until I've had my morning muffin," I said. "But, yes, that's fantastic news. Now, what's the bad news?"

She still looked slightly mystified that my reaction was so low-key, but she proceeded on. "Well, apparently, Malcolm was the guilty party. The prosecutor's office was getting ready to charge him, I guess, but he…"

I raised an eyebrow, waiting for her to go on. Malcolm met his demise, there was little doubt about that. I wondered how Charlotte managed to off him and make it look like an accident. Or a suicide.

"He?"

She narrowed her eyes. "Yes. You don't look at all surprised that Malcolm was guilty. All of us in this office were absolutely shocked to hear that. We were all shocked that one of our own was apparently the one who did this horrible thing."

"Well, you know, Cindy, I do have the gift of intuition. I kinda knew that there was something off about Malcolm."

She cocked her head. "Oh? And why did you come to work here if you thought our boss was so off?"

"I came to work here because this was an excellent opportunity. If I refused to work for every man who I thought was a bit of a jerk, I never would be able to work anywhere at all. Now, go on with your news about Malcolm."

"He's dead," she said. "He hung himself on a tree by his house."

Come on, Serena. Give her an Academy Award performance on this. She's dying for it. I dug in deep, and surprisingly enough, I was able to come up with the right emotion for hearing that Malcolm had died. It was genuine, too. I was sad, extremely sad, that it had come to this. He was a father and a husband, and I always got along with him. He did something extremely despicable, of course, and I knew that he wasn't going to have any other choice but to spend the rest of his miserable life in prison. Even so, I felt genuine sadness.

I shook my head, trying to dispel the tears in my eyes. "That's so awful," I said.

"Not so awful. I heard about what you did, throwing Malcolm under the bus to save the hide of your boyfriend. After that happened, it was only a matter of time before he would off himself. I think that you knew that when you did what you did."

"You're blaming me? Tell me that you wouldn't have done the exact same thing if you were defending an innocent man and you had exculpating evidence. If you're going to tell me that, then I have an ethics review that will have your name on it. That's pretty much criminal defense 101 – zealous advocacy for a client, any client, dictates that all exculpating evidence must be brought up in a timely manner. Even if that evidence implicates somebody else that you know."

"I know that. But, still, you could have given him a heads-up. Time to get his affairs in order."

I didn't say anything to her about the real reason why I couldn't possibly have given him any kind of heads-up. If I would have done that, then the first thing that Malcolm would have done would be to roll on Charlotte. If that would have happened, I would have been dead within the week. Cindy didn't know all the complicated transactions that went into my actions regarding Malcolm, and she really didn't need to know. She was, by far, the biggest gossip at the firm, not to mention the biggest pain in the ass.

"If I would have given him a heads-up, he probably would have fled. Now, could we please drop this? I have an entire roster of cases that I need to be attending to, not to mention several appellate briefs."

"Well, okay. I have some other news, too, if you would like to hear it."

I drew a breath. I was hoping against hope that the news that Cindy was about to tell me wasn't the news that I was expecting, although that didn't seem likely. "What's your other news?"

"There's a new guy who just started working here," she said, fanning herself. "And he's really cute." She put her fingers to her mouth in mock shame. "Did I just say that? I meant to say that he's a hot prospect. Worked in New York City, prosecuting Wall Street crooks. Now, here he is, on the other side. Former prosecutors are the best criminal defense attorneys, because they really know the system and how it works."

I swallowed, hard. "Is his name Derek, by any chance?"

"Yes. Derek Ripley. How did you know?"

My heart sank. It wasn't that I was taken aback by this news. It was quite the opposite – I had been bracing myself for it, ever since I saw that he was my new next-door neighbor, and that Charlotte had some evil plan to torment me. I had no idea, no clue, on how Charlotte had found out about what had happened between Derek and me, but it was clear that she knew everything. "He's living next door to me. His live-in girlfriend, Maggie, told me that he moved out here for a lucrative position. I guess I'm putting two and two together."

"Well, we're all going to lunch today to welcome him." She paused. "And I guess that Malcolm's funeral will be on Thursday. We're closing the office that day, so we're all expected to attend. I'm sure you don't want to, considering you're personally responsible for his demise, but I thought that I would give you a heads-up."

I threw down the pen that was in my hand and glared at Cindy. "Would you please stop saying that I'm personally responsible for Malcolm's death? How about saying that Malcolm is responsible for his own death? If he wouldn't have done what he did, then he wouldn't have been in the position that he was in – facing life in prison, if not the death penalty. All that I did was show the prosecutor that Malcolm was the one, because I refused to let Slade take the fall for what Malcolm did. Anybody in my shoes would do the same. Anybody with ethics, that is."

"Okay. But I wouldn't have done what you did. I'm more loyal than that."

"So, you would let an innocent man go to prison, just because somebody you knew was ultimately to blame? Read the book *The Count of Monte Cristo* and tell me how well that kind of scenario goes over with the innocent person." That was one of my favorite books growing up, and it told the tale of a boy who was railroaded into prison by various people, and how he got revenge upon them, one by one.

"I'm not familiar with that story," she said. "All that I know is that Malcolm is dead, and he wouldn't be if it weren't for you."

"Please leave my office," I told her. "Now."

She made a face and groaned. "Okay. Listen, you're expected to be at this lunch that we're having for the new guy. It's going to be at The Fish Market, and a table has already been reserved. I think that we're going to be talking about succession as well. Now that Malcolm is passed, we're all going to have to vote on who is going to be the next managing partner, and, quite frankly, there's been talk that this firm might be in trouble financially. That's just the rumor, but I've heard that Malcolm has been cooking the books because he has some serious gambling debts. We might all be looking for another job soon, and that will be on your head as well."

I nodded my head. It didn't surprise me – that Malcolm had gambling debts. It would actually explain a lot of things to me. Things that had nagged at me all along. Such as why

Malcolm would resort to murder, and how did he get involved with Charlotte in the first place? Could it be that he owed her family money, and Charlotte just had him do Sam's murder in lieu of paying them? That would be something that would make sense to me. If that was the case, I suddenly felt badly for Malcolm. Maybe he killed Sam out of sheer desperation, knowing that it was either Sam's life or his own. I never did quite buy the story that Malcolm only did that to Sam because he was up Charlotte's ass. That was part of it, no doubt, but I always thought that there had to be something more.

"Well, listen, if this firm was built upon a house of cards, which it certainly seemed to be if the managing partner had serious gambling debts, then it would have collapsed eventually anyhow. So, again, you can't blame me if this firm goes under. It would have only been a matter of time."

"You go on telling yourself that, if that's what you need to believe in order to sleep at night. In the meantime, I suggest that you try to be a part of the solution, assuming that there is one."

At that, she left, and I picked up the phone to call Slade. He picked up on the first ring.

"Serena," he said. "What's going on?"

"I have to attend a luncheon today to welcome the newest member of the firm."

"Let me guess. The new firm member's name is Derek."

"Damn, you're good. Listen, there's something else, too."

"What's that?"

"There's a rumor going around that Malcolm might not have been solvent. He possibly has some serious gambling debts. Can you find out something about that? I have this suspicion that another piece of the puzzle has been resolved."

Slade was quiet for just a few minutes. "That makes sense," he finally said. "Maybe he got involved with Charlotte because he needed money, and her family lent it to him."

"That's what I was thinking. Anyhow, find out for me."

"I will." He paused again. "Nothing has happened with my mother, although I've called the station, and, apparently, Hugh's case has been reopened. That's the word with the detective on my case, anyhow. He told me that the prosecutor is getting ready to drop the charges against me, and he also wanted to warn me that my mother is the prime suspect now in Hugh's disappearance. Just brace yourself."

"I will. I would imagine that, if she's arrested, you'll bail her out immediately, and then we'll go to work. In the meantime, I'm getting some experts lined up for her. I want to be ready to hit the ground running. Maybe we can even work some kind of deal with the prosecutor, if the evidence from the expert will be strong enough. We'll just have to see."

"Okay. Well, in the meantime, we're in a holding pattern with my mom. I'll find out what I need to find out about Malcolm and his gambling debts."

"Thanks."

I hung up the phone and put my head in my hands. There was a pile of files on my desk, files that I was going to have to soon review and start working. But I couldn't think about those. I could only think about how awful this luncheon was going to be, and how I was going to have to fake affection for this despicable Derek.

And I also couldn't get Cindy's words out my head. Was she right? Was I morally culpable for Malcolm's death?

Would Cindy really have let an innocent client go to prison to save Malcolm's neck, and, if so, did she really expect me to do the same thing?

I hated that Cindy was in my head-space in the way that she was. She was such a double-crossing snake, but yet, she held some degree of power in the office.

This was going to be a long day.

Chapter Four

We all met at The Fish Market right at noon. I was there as well, even though it was the last place I wanted to be. There was a long table that was reserved for the officers and partners of the firm. The associates weren't invited, except for me. I assumed I was only invited because everybody was going to try to pile on me for Malcolm's death. I wasn't going to have any of that, of course. I would just walk right out if anybody started to harass me for that.

I held my breath as I saw Derek stroll in. He seemed to be very friendly with everyone, because some people hugged him, and he was talking easily amongst everyone. I tried to avoid his eyes, but every time I looked at him, he was looking back at me.

To my dismay, he took a seat right next to me. "Hello again, Serena," he said. "We have to stop meeting this way."

I felt an icy chill run through my veins, as I remembered that was the phrase he had said to me at the cabin that one night. Almost word for word.

I took a sip of wine, as there were several bottles on the table, and I had poured myself a glass. "Don't think that I have forgiven you for what you did," I told him, between gritted teeth. "But you won't intimidate me now. I'm not that scared Goth chick that you took advantage of. Fair warning."

"Oh, I know. You have that beast on a leash. He does know how to throw an amazing left hook, I'll give him that. I've always had problems fighting lefties. Right-handed people often do."

"Yes. I have that beast on a leash." I didn't tell him that wasn't entirely accurate. After all, *I* was typically the one on the leash, not Slade. Of course, that wasn't something that I necessarily shared with anyone, let alone my tormentor.

He smiled at me, an amused smile that didn't show any hint of shame. Instead, it hinted of deviancy and evil. He took a sip of his wine as he continued to smile at me. I felt the icy-cold feeling in my veins, and I felt like I had to get out of that room.

I didn't leave the room, though, because this was going to be my life. I was going to have to somehow tolerate this man's presence if I was going to represent Margot.

"What is it that you think that I did to you years ago?" he asked me.

I didn't know what game he was playing. Did he want me to tell him, and that would somehow turn him on? Or did he honestly not remember? That was a possibility, as he was very drunk that night.

When I looked at his face, though, I knew that he knew what he did. There was no memory loss. In fact, by looking at him, I would say that he still replayed that scene in his mind, over and over again, and got a thrill out of it. I wondered if it was the only time that he had done something like that. Looking at his face, I seriously doubted that I was the only one. He just looked like the wrong kind of pervert, the kind who got his jollies by hurting women.

Cindy was watching, looking from me to Derek, and back again. I saw that her devious wheels were turning as she watched us, and I wanted to smack her. Hard. I wanted to use all the deadly force that I knew how to use with my hands, although that wasn't a lot. I was a runner, not a fighter, and I knew that. I had never hit another person in my life.

Maybe it was time that I learned how.

Once everyone got around the table, Harry, who was second-in-command to Malcolm, stood up. He clinked his glass with his spoon to get our attention, and everyone became silent. "I've gathered everyone here today to talk about the future of this firm, and to introduce you to the newest partner, Derek Ripley. Derek has come to us from New York City, where he was working for the DA's office. I've seduced him to the dark side, or, rather, Malcolm managed to seduce him." He looked sad.

We all raised our glasses in toast, and Harry continued on.

"As you probably know, we lost Malcolm, who was our founding father. Our firm will continue on without him, as I will be taking over his cases and his duties. My own cases, the ones that I was working on, will be evenly distributed amongst the rest of this team. We can have a smooth transition, because Malcolm prepared documents that would help ease the necessary growing pains that occur in situations such as this one." He sat down. "I'll be happy to entertain any questions that you have about this."

I played with my fork while I thought about what to ask

and how to ask it. Cindy had no such qualms, for she piped right up. "I have a question. I heard that Malcolm wasn't solvent, and that he was using the firm's funds for his own slush gambling fund. And that the firm isn't solvent now, either. I guess I need to ask if we all need to find another job."

Harry took a deep breath, and I closed my eyes and felt acute anxiety coming from him. I could feel his chest tightening and his heart start to race, and, as I felt his emotions flood through my own body, and I knew that I was going to have to speak with Slade about the firm. If there was the possibility that our firm was going under, would Charlotte still be as adamant that Slade's mother had to be represented by us? What would happen in case the firm fell?

That was an open question. I knew that Charlotte had stipulated that my firm had to represent Margot, and, apparently, that was because she wanted Derek working with me in close quarters. That was part of her plan to torment me. If the firm went belly-up, though, would she renege on the deal? If she did, I would be put into danger again. Her career would be ruined, because Slade would release those documents about her youth to the media contact he knew.

Harry took another deep breath and cleared his throat. "I'm not going to lie to you. I have been finding out some disturbing realities as I have been looking through Malcolm's books. He apparently was in debt to the Garancino family for quite a lot of money. With interest and penalties and all of that, it appears that his debt to that family was in the millions. I have an accountant who is trying to sort the entire thing out, even as we speak."

I cocked my head, wondering if anyone was going to

put two and two together. Everyone knew that Malcolm killed Sam. Nobody knew any motive. I wondered if anyone would figure out that Malcolm's debt to the Garancinos had anything at all to do with Sam's murder. If anyone figured that out, the trail would inevitably lead to Charlotte. That, of course, would be dangerous for me, because Slade said that if Charlotte ever got into trouble for what she did, she would have nothing to lose. Her family would then put a hit on me, and that would be it.

I drummed my fingers on the table, watching Derek and fantasizing about Derek and Charlotte being in the same car. In my mind's eye, I saw myself cutting the brakes of this car and the two of them careening off a cliff. That was an image that made me smile, I'm not going to lie.

"You ever go to the mountains?" I asked Derek, just out of the blue.

He gave me a weird look. "I haven't. I just got here. But I'm sure that I will. I'm looking into getting a place in Big Bear." Big Bear was a mountain resort that was just north of us. I had been up there in the wintertime, and it was freezing and snowing. It was a bit of a miserable experience for me, because I had grown accustomed to gorgeous year-round weather, but I went to hang out with Donny, whose cousin had a cabin up there.

As I drummed my fingers on the table some more, I barely listened to Harry. I knew what was going on, and I was going to have to talk to Slade about it. What I was doing, instead of listening to Harry, was furthering my fantasy. I had been up on the roads to Big Bear. I was surprised that there weren't more accidents, because those roads were winding and there were very few guard rails. The people who drove those roads weren't careful, either. They were people who drove those roads all the time, so, even when the conditions were poor, nobody really slowed down. It would be so easy for a car just to fall off that mountain, really. Just fall off the mountain…I wondered if cars exploded once they got to the bottom, like in the movies.

Harry brought me back into the conversation. "Serena, you've been quiet. What's on your mind?"

Seeing Derek burned alive as his car careens off a cliff and bursts into flames. "I guess I'm not surprised by any of this. Malcolm killed a man. That tells you right there that he was leading a double life. Gambling debts go right along with that, although I am surprised that he owed so much. How do you even gamble away millions? That's just beyond me."

Harry just shrugged his shoulders. "He was a high-roller. Apparently he was a VIP at many Vegas casinos, not to mention casinos in Monte Carlo. That's where he really got into trouble. He enjoyed playing high stakes wherever he went. I guess the gambling was an addiction, but so was the feeling of being important. He was treated like royalty at these casinos, apparently, and that must have been a real high for him as well." He shook his head. "At least, that's what my wife was telling me when I told her about Malcolm's problems. She's a therapist, and she treats people with addictions. She's seen gambling addicts, and they're addicted to the lifestyle that comes with the game, as much as they are addicted to the game itself. That said, he has also gotten into trouble with online gambling."

"I guess that answers my question."

Harry took another deep breath. "Serena, I need to speak with you alone."

I looked around the table at everyone who was looking at me with quizzical expressions. Nobody seemed to know what Harry needed to talk to me about.

"Okay," I said. I pointed to a table that was at the far end of the room. Harry had rented out the entire room of the restaurant, and I hoped that the table was far enough away that the others wouldn't be able to hear what we were talking about.

We went to the table, and I saw Cindy looking at us. She was dying to know what was being said, and I wondered if she knew how to read lips. She probably did – she was that nosy and that much up in everyone's business all the time. Lip-reading would be a skill that she would definitely be into. "What did you need to say to me?" I asked Harry.

"You're angry about Malcolm. I don't blame you. He apparently framed your...significant other. That's something that is pretty unforgivable."

"Yes, yes it is."

"I just wanted you to know that I get why you're angry with Malcolm. And I hope that it doesn't impair your relationship with the rest of us. We need you on our team, Serena, now more than ever. You're one of the best attorneys we have, even though you've technically not yet been an attorney with our firm. I'm sure you passed that bar with flying colors, though, so I'm not worried about that." He narrowed his eyes. "I'm quite sure that your special abilities come in handy when you're selecting a jury."

"Yes, yes they do," I said. That was the truth. I could pinpoint who was telling the truth on any given jury, and that skill was invaluable. That was the one thing that I had over most other attorneys.

"So, I guess what I'm trying to say is – please don't leave us. We're going to get through this mess with the gambling debts and insolvency. It won't be easy, but we'll get through it."

I nodded my head. "Okay. Is there anything else that you needed to say to me?"

"No."

At that, we went back over to the main table. He didn't know it, of course, but he really didn't need to give me that little pep talk. I was already committed to the firm, come hell or high water. We were going to represent Margot, after all, assuming that she was arrested for Hugh's murder.

Everybody gave their order to the waitress who had come around our table. Everyone ordered some kind of seafood, and I just ordered cucumber sushi rolls and a salad with vinegar and oil. There were times when I almost wished that I weren't a vegan – times when I saw everyone else indulging in what looked like amazing seafood was one of those times. I could never be tempted by pork or beef – I knew those animals, cows and pigs, and I knew that they had emotions just like humans. I couldn't imagine eating them. But fish...that was kind of a different story. Nonetheless, I didn't want any creature to give his life for me, so I just didn't go there.

There was plenty of wine to go around, even though it technically was in the middle of the work day. I guess nobody really cared all that much, as our office building was within walking distance of this particular restaurant and most of us actually did walk. Some people took their cars, which was silly. Others hailed a pedi-cab, which were ubiquitous in downtown San Diego. These were little cabs that were driven by boys and girls on bicycles. I used to call them rickshaws, because that was what they reminded me of – rickshaws that I used to see in old books about China. I half thought that I would see Donny or Michael on one of those things, because that seemed to be what they would really like to be doing – enjoying the sunshine, getting some exercise, all while getting paid. They would say that was the life for them.

While everyone else was actively trying to get to know the new guy, while gossiping and fretting about the future of our firm, I sat back and silently watched all my co-workers. I didn't have a word to say to Derek, of course. He kept looking over at me, and he made my skin crawl every time. I tried not to feel the icy feeling of panic and fear, but, every so once in awhile, those feelings crept back in. I shook off those feelings and soldiered on.

The food came, and I dug in while drinking more wine. I was going to end up stumbling back to my job at that rate, but so was everyone else. By the looks of things, everyone was trying to forget about the fact that the firm was on its last legs, thanks to Malcolm, by drinking a shit-ton of wine. What did concern me was that Derek was drinking wine, right along with the rest of the people, and I thought I saw him leering at me.

He put his hand on my leg, and I thought I was going to vomit. I swallowed hard as he leaned down and said "you know, you grew up to be really hot. I mean, you were smoking in high school. That's why I wanted you back then. I hope that you know that. But the way you look now..." He whistled low. "I could really hit that."

I swallowed hard, and firmly attempted to move his hand from my leg, but I couldn't. The more I tried to get his hand off of me, the harder he gripped. All at once, it all came flooding back to me. The way he was holding onto me, even though I was trying to get away, brought it all back to me. I found myself involuntarily making a fist and punching him, right in the face.

I looked around and noticed that everyone had stopped talking and drinking, and were just staring right at me.

Derek had finally taken his hand off of my leg, as he rubbed his face and glared at me. I said nothing, but just got up and went to the bathroom with my purse.

Halfway there, I decided I didn't want to go to the bathroom. I wanted out of this place. I needed out. I was shaking all over, and tears were streaming down my face. I found our waiter, explained the situation, and asked for my bill. He brought it out, I gave him my credit card, which he processed, and then I just left.

I left the restaurant and got to the street. There were hundreds of people walking around, because it was lunchtime. I could have just walked over to my office, as it was extremely close, but I decided against that. I didn't want to go back there, and I didn't want to go home. I hadn't yet moved in with Slade, although he was asking me to, especially since Derek was living right next door to me. I didn't feel right doing that, though. Not like this. When I lived with him, it would be because I wanted to live with him, not because I had to. I didn't like the feeling that I was forced into living with Slade before we were ready to make that step. So, thus far, I had refused him on this. I didn't mind staying with him for a period of time, but actually moving in with him - I wasn't there yet.

Besides, he currently had his mother staying with him. I didn't want to move in there while she was there, especially since her case was still so up in the air.

I finally ended up walking into a bar in the Gaslamp District. It was an Irish pub, so it was dark and woody inside. The waitress came around and I ordered a dirty martini and some peanuts. I then called Slade, who picked up on the first ring.

"Hey," he said. "I've been thinking about you. How are things going over there?"

"Not good. Listen, I need to talk to you. I'm kinda drunk, though, so I can't drive to where you are."

"Where are you? I'll be there as soon as I can."

I gave him the name of the bar, and he told me to sit tight, for he would be driving to meet me soon.

I tapped my fingers on the bar, wondering about a multitude of things. Slade was about to be cleared by the prosecutor, which was wonderful. As soon as the charges were dropped, I would imagine he would want to return to his home in LA. He had a business to run, a business that he hadn't paid enough attention to while this whole murder thing was going on. He had a large, beautiful mansion on one of the Malibu cliffs. He had a whole life up there, a life that I wasn't a part of.

So, there was that. We hadn't yet talked about that - about what life was going to be like once things were settling in for him back at his home. It was unspoken that he was going to have to do something – either return back to LA to resume his life, or sell everything and move down here. He could very easily open up another location for his firm right here in San Diego, but I didn't want to ask that of him. Logistically, it would be a nightmare, since all of his scientists and talent were in LA.

There was also the matter of his mother, and the matter of my firm possibly going belly-up. That was complicated, too, since his mother would be charged in LA for the murder of Hugh. She was staying with him down here, and her firm, the one that she would have to go to, which was my firm, was here as well. But she was going to have to travel to LA to get things done in her case. So would I.

And the firm…I shook my head. If it went insolvent, then what? Would Charlotte be satisfied if Margot was going to have to be represented by somebody else? What was with that whole deal, anyhow, unless she just wanted to make sure that I stayed at the firm with Derek there? Maybe that was the only reason why she stipulated that my firm represent Margot, and I was reading too much into it.

I drank one dirty martini, and then another, while waiting for Slade to arrive, and I was starting to really feel it. I got up to use the restroom, and my legs felt like they weren't quite a part of the rest of my body. Everyone there seemed like they were at the end of a long tunnel, and nothing seemed quite real.

When I came back out, Slade was standing there at the bar, looking around. I waved and he saw me and came right over. "Serena, you don't look so good," he said, putting his hand on the small of my back. "Here, let me help you over to your seat."

"I'm good," I said, knowing that I was slurring my words. I sat down and he sat down right next to me. He put his arm around me and put his finger on my chin. I looked right at him, and I felt immediately calmed. He had that effect on me – whenever I was around him, I felt like my best self. No matter what was happening in my life, I felt elevated whenever he was in my presence.

"So," he said, with a slight smirk on his face. "Drunky, what is that you wanted to talk to me about?" His smirk turned into a look of amusement, as if he had never seen me this drunk. I guessed it was because he never actually had seen me this drunk.

"Oh, god, I have so much on my mind right now. The prosecutors will be dropping the charges against you, which is awesome, of course. But what happens next? We haven't talked about that, oh, and my firm might be going belly-up because Malcolm had some serious gambling debts. Bet you can't guess who he owed a lot of money to?"

"Wait. Hold on, one topic at a time. Now, on the subject of what I'm going to do, now that the charges against me will be dropped – I've thought about that, and I realize that I probably need to be around here for a little while. At least until my mother's case is resolved. After all, her law firm is located down here. I have an interim team in place at my corporation, and, thus far, they're doing a great job. I do plan to go back to being the active CEO there, of course, once the dust settles down here. The board has agreed to that arrangement, so I should be fine for a little while down here."

I nodded my head, feeling clingy right at that moment. "And what happens to us when you go back to LA?"

He just kind of stared at me when I said that, and then he looked at the bar. "What was the other thing that you were going to ask me about? Malcolm had some serious gambling debts with the Garancinos? You told me some-thing about that over the phone, and I haven't had the chance to follow up on it. Tell me what you know."

"Um," I said, suddenly feeling that I was losing my train of thought. I asked him a direct question about what was going to happen with the two of us when he went back to LA, and he completely avoided it. I hated that he did that, but, more than that, I felt just a little bit panicky. Why wouldn't he answer that question? It was a straightforward question that demanded an answer that was just as straight-forward. Yet he avoided it. Why?

He sat there, looking at me patiently. "You were saying something about the firm going belly-up because Malcolm had gambling debts. What's going on with that?"

I shook my head. "Yes. Malcolm had tremendous gambling debts. I guess that he was a high-roller in Vegas and Monte Carlo. He was a high-roller on the Garancino's dime, apparently. We all know what happens when you get in over your head with the mob."

"Yes. You end up doing jobs for them or you end up at the bottom of the ocean with cement shoes. One of the two. I guess that Malcolm chose option number one, which is why he killed Sam. But he still has existing debts with them? I would have thought that his killing Sam would have wiped the slate clean."

"Apparently not. Perhaps that act just wiped part of the slate clean, not the whole slate. Which brings me to the inescapable conclusion that Malcolm must have been way, way, way over his head with those people. I'm surprised that Charlotte never said anything to you about all of that."

Slade shook his head. "She wouldn't say anything to me about that. I'm sure that that piece of information was between her and Malcolm. It was a business transaction for her, nothing more. Why would she confide in me about that?"

"Good point." I fidgeted with my water glass a little bit, and then took a tiny sip. I wanted to bring up to Slade the fact that he avoided the LA question, but, for some reason, I was nervous to do so. I was nervous, I guessed, because I really didn't want to know what his answer was for this. I didn't want to hear from him that he was going back to LA and would forget all about me.

I silently cursed myself again about being "that girl." That girl whose imagination ran wild with speculation about what was going to happen in the future with her guy. Slade had upended me completely, body and soul, and there was no coming back from that. I imagined that, if he just went on his merry way back to his home in LA, and just left me here, forgotten, I would give up on men for a little while. Maybe forever. It just wasn't worth it to put my heart out there and have it stomped on. Of course, the major problem was that Slade wasn't the first person to stomp on my heart. He wasn't even close. I had been beaten down so many times, and I always, always got right back up.

I felt the refrains of the song *I Will Survive* in my head as I tentatively asked him to answer my earlier question. "Slade, I asked you earlier what you thought would happen with us when you went back to LA. You avoided that question." I looked up at him shyly from behind my water glass, and then took another sip.

He took my hands. "I don't think that far, Serena," he said. "I have to put one foot in front of the other right now. I've just come out of a period in my life where I was sure I would spend the rest of it in prison, only to become worried that it's my mother who will spend the rest of her life in prison. It's funny how certain things that were so important before – things like running my business and making it the international conglomerate that it is – become less so when you're faced with what really matters."

I nodded my head and said nothing. I was hoping that he would give me the answer that I really wanted to hear, but, thus far, he wasn't giving me that at all. He wasn't giving me anything.

"Listen," he said. "I will make a small commitment to you, although it's probably not what you're looking for. I'll buy your firm. I'm quite sure that your now-top partner there, Harry, will be perfectly willing to negotiate with me. I can make the whole thing solvent again."

I had mixed emotions about him doing that. I knew that he had the money for it, but, at the same time, I didn't know why he was doing it. Was it because he needed the firm for Margot, or because he didn't want me to lose my job?

I shook my head. "I'm becoming somebody I don't want to be," I said quietly.

He put his hand on mine. "What do you mean?"

"Insecure. Needy. I'm not that girl, but you keep me so off-balance."

He looked mystified that I was talking this way. "I guess I don't understand. I thought you would be happy that your firm wouldn't be going bankrupt."

"I am." That was all that I said. It was time to change the subject, and change it quickly. I wasn't going to be the interrogator here. "Well, you might buy the firm, but I might not be working there much longer."

Slade's face crinkled when I said that. "What do you mean?"

"I punched Derek today at the luncheon that our firm had in his honor. He put his hand on my leg and…"

Telling Slade about this was a mistake. He immediately clenched his fist and had a look on his face that told me he was about to kick some ass. Again. "Excuse me," he said, getting up. "I'm so sorry, Serena, but I hope that you're done with your dirty martini. Because I'm going to pay the bill, and we're getting out of here."

"Where are we going?" I asked, getting up. I knew the answer to that question, of course. It was obvious. There was going to be some kind of cage match between Slade and Derek, and I wasn't going to be happy about it. "Slade, you're still technically out on bail, at least until the prosecutor completely drops the charges against you. I would suggest that-"

My words were falling on deaf ears. Slade was striding purposefully through the bar, he found a barmaid and gave her some money. Then he turned around, and put his arm around me. "Steady on your feet, my beautiful drunk Serena. We're going to your home."

I shook my head. I didn't want to face Derek, not that soon.

However, I knew that if I protested, my words would continue to fall on deaf ears.

Slade had a look in his eye that was murderous.

I wondered what he was truly capable of.

Chapter Five

Slade

We got out into the street, and I put Serena gently into the front seat of my Tesla and strapped her in. She was like a rag doll by then, full of gin martinis. That was just as well, as I hoped that she wouldn't understand what was about to go down. I loved this woman, and I had intended to marry her, but I wanted it to be a complete surprise. That was why I kept avoiding her questions about the future. I hated that she was kept off-balance, but I really wanted to see a look of total shock on her face when I finally bended down on one knee with the biggest, and most beautiful, rock I could possibly find.

Because I wanted her to be my wife, it gave me all the more reason to protect her. I was going to have to kick some ass, and I was going to have to kick it well this time. I had warned Derek, when I confronted him on his porch that morning, to stay the hell away from Serena. He apparently didn't heed my warning, so I was going to have to go to step

2. It wasn't necessarily something that I wanted to do, but sometimes you have to do what you have to do.

I tried not to drive like a maniac, because I knew that Serena wasn't feeling so good. She was crumpled up against the door and was holding her belly. "Honey, just let me know if you start to feel sick," I told her. I had been there too many times before – drinking too much and feeling like crap. It wasn't even like her to drink this much, but I guessed that Derek just had that effect on her. She probably drank like that to try to escape how she felt around that jackass. I knew that Charlotte's whole game was to make sure that Derek psychologically tortured Serena, but I was goddamned if he was ever going to lay a hand on her again.

We got to her house, and I helped her inside her door. "Slade, I don't want to be here," she said. "I can't be here. I don't want to be near that man. That awful man."

"Shhh," I said. "We won't be staying long. We'll go back to my house soon. But I have to take care of something here." I laid her gently down on her couch and put a blanket over her. Her dogs weren't there, of course, because they were staying with me. I found myself wishing that her dogs were around, though, because I knew how much comfort Serena drew from them.

I then went out the door and headed next door. I pounded on the door, and a petite blonde woman answered. She looked me up and down and smiled. "Hi, can I help you?"

"I need to speak with Derek."

At that, Derek himself appeared directly behind her. His face furrowed, and he shoved blondie to the side. "I can take care of this, Maggie. Why don't you go back into the kitchen and continue chopping onions?"

She looked at me quizzically and then looked very worried. "Be careful," she whispered to him.

Derek said nothing, but just continued to stand there. As soon as Maggie disappeared into the kitchen though, he came out on the porch. "I knew that you would be back here," he said. "I knew it."

I clenched my fist. "If you knew this, then why would you do what you did?" I then hauled off and hit him right in the gut, and then rapidly punched him in the face. I had learned how to fight when I was very young, before I was taken in by Helen and Scott. I secretly was learning because I wanted to take on my father one day and make sure he never laid another hand on my mother. Of course, she took care of my father before I had the chance to, but the fighting lessons had always stuck with me.

You can take a boy from the street, but you may never take the street from the boy.

Derek crumpled on the porch again. I knew his soft spot and this was crucial. A good fighter always knows his opponent's weaknesses before even throwing a punch. It was fairly easy to find Derek's.

He stumbled back up on his feet, but I could tell that he didn't have much fight in him that night. That was possibly a good thing, because maybe I could keep him in line without resorting to Plan B. He shook his head. "Man, I was drinking today. Probably drinking a bit too much. It won't happen again."

Typical bully. He was all bluster until somebody gives him a beat-down. He was a marshmallow inside, and I was able to completely exploit this.

"Good. Listen. If I hear one more word from Serena about you harassing her, I'll have to go to the next step. And I can guarantee that you won't like the next step."

"I'm sure I won't, but tell me what this next step would be."

I narrowed my eyes. "Let's just say that I know where to hide the body." I had done it before, when I helped my mother cover-up the homicide of Hugh. I did it so well, in fact, that Hugh was never found at all. He was fish food and Derek would be too if he continued harassing Serena.

Actually, I had no idea if I actually would be capable of killing this man in cold blood. I certainly would be if he attacked Serena sexually again. I had never come close to killing anyone in my life, but this man was somebody who would bring that out in me. I told Serena over and over again that any man is capable of anything, and I did believe that.

But I hoped that merely threatening him would be enough for him to back the hell off.

"You're actually threatening to kill me?"

I simply raised an eyebrow. "Either that or expose you for what you are. I won't even say that I'm going to expose you for who you are, because you're not even human to me. You're an ant. You're somebody who deserves to be crushed under my heel. And you will be, trust me, you will be, if you ever lay another hand on Serena."

"You got no proof of nothing."

"Oh, don't I?" There was some way that Charlotte had found out about Derek's connection to Serena, and I knew what it was. There had to have been some medical record out there that tied Serena and Derek together. Serena didn't say as much, but I suspected that she did seek help for her miscarriage, and that she put Derek's name down as the possible father of that baby. Not that this mattered, though. This slime would just say that it was consensual sex and no one would be the wiser. That's what made rape such a terrible crime to try to prosecute, I would imagine – too much "he said - she said," to substantiate anything. And, well, trying to report Derek's crime at this late date wouldn't do much good. The Statute of Limitations had probably passed.

"No, you don't," he said.

I stood right in front of him, my fists clenched, and just stared him down. I hoped that intimidating him would be enough for him to leave Serena alone. He already knew that I could throw a punch and that I could take his punches very well. He crossed his arms in front of his chest, but, after a few minutes of my staring him down, he dropped his arms to his side and looked away.

That was what I needed to see. I needed to see that he was going to submit, and that's exactly what he did. He was like a little dog that rolled on his back, which was the dog's way of pleading not to be hurt. It was a dog's way of submitting.

I narrowed my eyes and continued to stare at him for a little while longer, and then I pointed at him. "Leave her the fuck alone," I said. "Or you'll see what is coming to you, and it won't be pretty. As I said, I know where to hide a body."

At that, Maggie reappeared on the porch. "I have dinner cooking," she said. "Would you like to join us? And you're with Serena, aren't you? I would love it if you and she both could join us. I'd like to be friends."

I put my hand behind my neck, and Derek was staring at the floor. Maggie was looking from Derek to me and back again, sensing that there was tension between the two of us, but not really understanding why. "I would love to stay for dinner," I said, still staring at the cowed Derek. "But I don't think that Serena is up to it. She's not feeling well. Can we take a rain check, though?"

Maggie nodded her head. "I'm a great cook," she said. "I know that Serena is a vegan, but still, I think that I could probably accommodate her. Derek here eats only meat and some potatoes. Getting him to eat veggies has been a totally uphill and useless battle. I can't get him to even try a vegetable. But I know how to cook them very well. It would be nice to actually serve somebody who can appreciate that."

I smiled at her. She seemed like a sweet person. Why she was wrapped up with this Derek character, I didn't know. I wondered why anyone would be involved with such a creep.

"I'll be sure and tell Serena about your cooking skills. I'm sure she would love to come and visit you guys," I said, trying to be nice. Of course, Serena wasn't going to want to have dinner with these two, and I wouldn't ask her. But I didn't want to insult sweet Maggie.

The three of us stood awkwardly on the porch for a beat, and then I begged off. "Well, I have to go back to check on Serena. She's not feeling well."

"Tell her that we're thinking of her," Maggie said. "And we hope that she can make it over here soon."

"I will," I said, nodding my head.

And then I went back to check on Serena at her home right next door.

Chapter Six

Serena

I lay on the couch, but the room was spinning. It was like a fast carousel. I closed my eyes, feeling that nothing was real. Was there really an evil man living right next door? The man who had haunted my dreams ever since I was 17 years old? The man who took my virginity and just left me in the woods after he was through with me? And Slade, apparently, was right next door. I didn't know what he was going to do to Derek, and I didn't really want to find out.

Thankfully, Slade didn't take too long. He was back with me within an hour. He came over to me, where I was lying on the couch, hugging a large pillow to my stomach. He smoothed back my hair. "You feeling a bit better?" he asked me.

I shook my head. "I'm feeling really pukey right now, but I don't know if I can get up off this couch to do anything about it."

At that, Slade got up and went into the kitchen. He

returned a few moments later with some aspirin, a large jug of water and another glass that had soda water and bitters in it. "Here," he said, making me sit up. "Take these aspirin and drink all of this water down - every bit of this water. And, after you drink all of this water, take the soda and bitters. Trust me, you'll thank me in the morning."

I took the aspirin and contemplated the jug of water. It was a huge jug, probably holding about 64 oz of water. It was the jug that I took to the gym when I lifted weights and knew I'd be sweating a lot. I didn't know how I was possibly going to down all of that water, on top of all the alcohol that I already had swimming around in my belly. Still, I knew that Slade was right – this water and aspirin were the best things for me right at that moment.

"You're really good to me," I said to him. "Why are you so good to me?"

"Now, Serena, you're not sounding like yourself. You know why I'm good to you." He kissed me on the forehead lightly. "Don't you?"

I nodded my head, but I didn't really know. I didn't know much at that moment. Well, I knew that the room was spinning and that Slade didn't exactly seem real, but that was all that really popped into my brain. "Yes," I said weakly.

He smoothed my hair once more and kissed me on the forehead again. "I'm good to you because I'm crazy about you. I don't think that you know how crazy I am about you. But I am. You get me, more than anybody else ever has."

I blinked. "But I don't understand. You're leaving me aren't you? Your life isn't here, it's in LA. You have to return to that life, don't you? I mean, I guess we could see each other on the weekends, some weekends, but I don't know. I never contemplated being in a commuter relationship."

I was hoping that he would give me some indication, any indication, on what he wanted to do when he went back to his LA home. But he still didn't. He just continued to stare at me and urging me to keep drinking the water. "Let's not think about all of that," he said to me. "It's far in the future, maybe. Remember, my mom is being represented by your firm, so I need to be around for that. I need to make sure that she gets out of killing Hugh."

I put my hand on his arm and touched it lightly. "You feel responsible, don't you? Somehow?"

He sighed and stared at the wall. His hands were clenched together in front of him, and then he hung his head. "Yes. I do." He took a deep breath. "I do. I should have thought things through that night a little better. But I didn't. I went on auto-pilot. I should have been thinking about the impact Charlotte would have on my life when she knew what happened to Hugh. What kind of impact she would have when she knew what mom and I did to Hugh's body."

I continued to stroke his arm lightly while I drank my water. "You did what you thought was best in that situation. You were young, very young. And you panicked. I probably would have done the same exact thing in that situation. If Luke or my father or Christopher were in that situation, I probably would have done the same thing. So, please, don't blame yourself."

"I know. But my mother would have done anything that I asked her to in that situation. If I just would have asked her to turn herself in, she would have done it. But I didn't. Maybe it would have been better if she would have turned herself in. I don't know. What I do know is that it's not only come back to bite me in the ass, but it has also given Charlotte ammunition against me all these fucking years. All these fucking years. The chickens are finally coming home to roost, I guess, so all these years that she's blackmailed me seem like a waste. I probably should have just gone to the police instead of giving Charlotte that kind of power over me."

It wasn't like Slade to be so questioning of his actions. Usually, he just plowed right through problems like they weren't even there. He was human, though, and, as such, he questioned whether he did the right thing. It was impossible to know, though, if he had done the right thing in this case. It was impossible to know because the alternative wasn't clear. Maybe Margot could have gotten away with it, on a self-defense claim, but maybe not. She probably wasn't able to afford a lawyer back then, and Slade wasn't able to help her get a good lawyer, because he was still in school and his adoptive parents didn't approve of him seeing Margot. Now, Margot definitely had the money for a decent attorney, because Slade had more money than Croesus.

"Well, Slade, there's not a lot of room for regret here. We just have to hope for the best. Hope that the police decide not to charge her, and, if she is charged, hope that we can get her off with a self-defense claim. There's not much else that we can do."

He nodded his head. "You're the drunk one, yet you're making more sense right now than I am." He looked at me with admiration in his beautiful green eyes. "Come on, let's go to my house. Your dogs are waiting for you there. My mom is there, too, of course, but I'm in the process of buying her a home around here."

I smiled. "What are you going to do with all these San Diego homes once you go back to LA?"

He shrugged. "Sell them. That's not a huge deal, is it?"

"No." I should have said that it was a huge deal for

99.9999% of the population, and only the truly wealthy could just buy and sell San Diego homes as if they were used books. "I guess it's not a huge deal to you."

At that, he gave me his hand. "Come, let's get you into my car and get you to my home. I'll call the firm tomorrow and tell them that you can't come in. Something tells me that the firm won't object to that, because, after all, I'm literally going to own that firm by the end of the week."

"Okay. But I don't want preferential treatment. That's the last thing I need – everybody going around and undermining me because I'm fucking the boss. I've always managed to get everywhere I need to be just by my ingenuity and brains. I'm not about to let nepotism sink me now."

"Deal. Now come, beautiful Serena. Let's get to my house and I'll tuck you into bed with your two girls. Hopefully you won't feel like crap tomorrow, but, from the looks of things, I hate to say it but…you're going to feel like shit. It's just inevitable, unfortunately. I should really develop a drug that cures hangovers. I could make a mint on that, don't you think?"

"Oh, god yes. A true hangover cure would be something that everyone would want."

I finished the rest of the water and took the soda and bitters.

Slade took my hand as we went to his car and then we headed to his place.

I had to think that this was the best thing right at that moment. Eventually, I would have to return back to my own home, and I was going to have to face Derek every single day at work, but, just for now, I felt safe and secure. I was going home with Slade.

Chapter Seven

When we got to Slade's house, the first thing that he noticed was that Margot wasn't there. We had some take-out food that we had picked up at a local Vietnamese restaurant. Pho was one of Margot's favorite dishes. Slade went to her room, and she wasn't there. Then he looked all around the house and the backyard, and she wasn't there, either.

"What's going on?" I asked him. I was anxious to start eating, because I knew that if I ate, my hangover in the morning would be alleviated greatly.

Slade's face was pale. "I need to make a phone call," he said. "If mom isn't here, there's a reason. She doesn't have a car."

I drew a breath. That didn't sound good at all. "Okay."

Slade went into the next room, and he was in there for awhile. When he came back out, he looked slightly better than he did before he went in. "Well, it's bad, but it isn't as bad as it could be."

I nodded. I knew what he was thinking – the worst-case scenario was that Charlotte decided to nab Margot. That wasn't on Slade's radar, I knew, but it didn't mean that it wouldn't happen. Another thing was that, somehow, someway, Margot ended up in the hospital. She was sick, even if she wasn't dying, as she had previously believed.

Those scenarios were unlikely, though. The most likely scenario was that Margot was taken into custody, and that was what I thought had happened.

Slade confirmed this for me. "Mom is up in LA, answering questions. At least, she's en route there." He sat down on the couch and put his head in his hands. "I was hoping that perhaps they wouldn't find the evidence to charge her. They still might not, but it doesn't look good."

"Is she in custody or is she a person of interest and is going up there voluntarily?" That was important, as I needed to be there with her if she was in custody. Slade and I had already explained to her that she needed to not answer any questions at all unless I was there as her attorney. If she went voluntarily and was not being detained, then she wouldn't have her Miranda rights read to her, and they really wouldn't attach. That's only if she was free to leave on her own volition.

"She's in custody, according to the station manager there in LA. Even if she weren't, we need to be there. I mean, you need to be there." He put his arm around me. "You're sober enough to do this, aren't you?"

"Yes. I mean, I will be if I can eat this food."

"Eat it in the car."

At that, we got into his car, putting Bella and Gigi in their carrier, and headed to LA. I dug into my food, which was in a little Chinese takeout box, using my chopsticks that were provided by the restaurant. "I'm sorry to be eating while you're driving," I said. "You must be starved."

He shook his head. "I'll grab a bite while you're in the

custody room with my mom. That's not important right now. What's important is that we get up there soon. Now, tell me about the Miranda warning thing. Are you saying that if mom isn't in custody, but she is free to leave, that she doesn't have a right to an attorney?"

"That's right, but anything she says in that situation would still be used against her in a court of law. But the police have to make it clear that she's not being charged, she's only being questioned as a person of interest, and that she is free to leave at any time. So, just because she's in custody doesn't mean that she's actually in custody sometimes. If that makes any sense at all."

"Of course it does. I suppose that's what happens when the media talks about a person of interest in a crime. They're only calling a person a 'person of interest' because they want to be able to talk to that person without a lawyer being present. That's pretty underhanded, though, if you ask me. If you're being questioned, you should have a right to have counsel present, period."

"I agree there completely, but it's one way of getting around the Miranda warnings. I mean, that happened to you when you were taken into custody, right? They told you that you were only being questioned and you were free to leave at any time?"

"Yeah, but I'm much more savvy than my mother is. I understand how important it is to have counsel with me when I'm being interrogated. Of course, at that time, I didn't quite understand all that was happening with Charlotte and Malcolm and all of that. It all came much later."

"Well at that time, when you were first being questioned, you didn't have the right to ask for your attorney."

"I didn't dream that I would need one at that time. How wrong I was. I couldn't imagine that anybody would have ever thought that I was actually guilty of killing Sam. Of course, once I found out what the true story was – that Charlotte was framing me for rejecting her, and that I couldn't do a thing about it unless I wanted to throw my mom under the bus – I knew that it never mattered anyhow whether I had a lawyer or not."

We drove up the coast while I ate my Pho with a pair of chopsticks. It was delicious and vegan-friendly. It was just vegetable broth, noodles and lots of Asian veggies, but it was really making me feel better. More coherent. That was important, too, because I couldn't properly represent Margot unless I had my faculties about me.

Slade was quiet for about an hour, and I wondered what was on his mind. I put my hand on his hand, and he smiled. "You know, Serena, I don't think that I ever properly thanked you for saving my hide. I'm sort of glad that you forced my hand on this, because it wasn't as bad as I imagined it would be."

"What do you mean by that?"

"Well, I imagined that if something happened and I didn't take the fall for Jordan's murder, then you would be dead and my mother would be in prison. Turns out that Charlotte was willing to deal after all, which kind of surprised me. I guess it's important to her that she achieve her Hollywood dream, and that's even more important to her than sticking it to me."

"But she did stick it to you if your mother is in custody for Hugh's murder."

"Yeah, but it could have been much, much worse. If she wasn't willing to deal at all, you would be dead right now. I have to keep reminding myself that. My mother is important, don't get me wrong, but you're the most important person in my life right now."

That felt warm to me, him saying that. Even if I had my doubts that we had a future together, it felt right that he was in love with me right at that moment. "I don't understand, though. Every time I ask you about what your long-term plans are, you change the subject."

He sighed. "I know. But I really need to get through this next part of my life before I can make any plans. I hope that you understand that. I know that's not what you wanted to hear, but…"

"Okay." It wasn't okay at all, but I knew where he was coming from.

We got to the station, and I was feeling much more sober and on my feet. Slade was waiting for me in the SUV, and I saw him get the two dogs out so he could walk them.

I was ready to tackle whatever the police were going to throw at me and at Margot. I introduced myself to the dispatcher, explained who I was, and she nodded and led me back to the interrogation room.

As I went back there, I looked back at Slade. His hands were shoved in his pockets and his eyes were downcast. I wanted to reassure him that I got this. I was going to make sure that this first interrogation went well, so that Margot didn't say anything that would come back to haunt her later. As I caught his eye, I knew that he had complete confidence in me. He nodded to me and I nodded back and went in.

Margot was sitting across from a very intimidating police-man. They were just sitting there, not saying a word, and, when Margot saw me, she got up and gave me a long spontaneous hug. "Thank goodness you're here," she said in a low voice. "I wanted to call Slade and tell him what was happening, but they didn't let me. They just came to the house and…" At that, she started to cry.

"Can you give us a minute?" I asked the cop.

"Just," he said. "I'll be back in one minute."

I sat down across from the crying Margot. "Okay, I'm here. You didn't say anything to that cop, did you?"

"No. I told him that I had the right to an attorney, just like you and Slade told me to say. The cop told me that I didn't have that right, because I wasn't being charged with anything. They only want to question me, he said, and he told me that I was free to leave at any time."

"Bastard." I hated that cops played that game. Pretend that the person really wasn't in custody, so they could get incriminating statements to nail them. "What did you say when the cop told you that?"

"I told him that I wanted my attorney anyhow, and that I wasn't going to say one word until you got here. Of course, the cop didn't actually let me call you. If Slade didn't call, I probably would be sitting here for days, silent as a church mouse, because I wasn't going to give them anything that they can use to hang me later."

"Good thinking. You're doing good." I held her while she cried some more. "You're going to be fine. I promise you. You're in good hands." I realized that I was saying the word "good" over and over, but that was the one word that came into my head. It was a generic word, too generic to really be reassuring, but I hoped that Margot was reassured anyhow.

The cop came back in one minute, just like he said he would. "Okay, you must be Serena Roberts. Margot here said that she wasn't going to say a word until you arrived. Now you're here, so let's get to work. I don't have all night for this."

"Of course, sir, you must be very busy," I said to him. I shot Margot a look because her facial expression told me that she wanted to kill this cop. Not that I blamed her. It was a dirty trick to tell her that she wasn't in custody simply because he wanted to make sure she didn't have her counsel there right away. It was a dirty trick in my opinion, but, unfortunately, was something that happened too often.

"I am very busy. So, let's get this show on the road. Margot, as I told you when I came to your son's house to pick you up, this department received an anonymous tip that you were responsible for the death of Hugh Robbins. After our department received this tip, we were able to obtain a search warrant of your former apartment in the Watts District of Los Angeles. This was the apartment that this tip indicated the homicide occurred. We were able to find blood splatters in this apartment which were picked up with our infrared devices. The tip plus the blood splatters in your former apartment have given this department probable cause to detain you for questioning."

"Officer O'Malley," I said, reading his name-tag, "It sounds to me like you were always planning to charge Ms. Facinelli. You just used the term 'probable cause.'"

"Yeah, what of it?"

"You told Ms. Facinelli that she was simply being brought in for questioning, not that she was being forcibly detained. You skirted the requirement that she be read her Miranda Rights, so I suggest that you do so right now."

He gave me a dirty look and shook his head. "Okay. Ms. Facinelli, you are under arrest for the homicide of Hugh Robbins. You have the right to remain silent. Anything you say can and will be held against you. You have a right to an attorney. If you cannot afford an attorney, one will be appointed for you. Do you understand these rights?"

"Yes," Margot said, looking at me with wide eyes. I patted her hand, and saw that she had tears in her eyes. "I understand your honor."

The cop snorted. "I thank you for calling me your honor, but I'm not that. I'm just a detective who needs to hear, from your own mouth, what happened with Hugh Robbins."

She took a deep breath and proceeded to tell Office O'Malley what happened. He wrote down everything she said. I let her speak, because I wanted to the details of what happened to get out into the open. She just needed to get it out there, and I would deal with it from that point on.

After she told the officer everything about Hugh - about how they went out, they came back to her home, she didn't ask him to come up, yet he ended up in her apartment anyhow - the officer asked her some questions.

"Okay, so, you shot this Hugh Robbins because you felt threatened by him. Is that correct?"

She looked over at me, and I nodded at her. "Yes. I felt very threatened. He wasn't supposed to be in my apartment at all." She started to tell him why she felt so threatened, but I put my hand on her hand, which was my way of telling her she was saying too much. She immediately clammed up when I did that.

The officer leaned back in his chair. "Help me understand. Why didn't you just confront him and ask him to leave?"

She shook her head. "I panicked. That's all that I can say."

He sighed. "You're not giving me much to go on here. Listen, Ms. Facinelli, you seem like a kind person. You don't seem much like a killer to me. There must be some reason why you would shoot first and ask questions later. Literally."

She looked over at me, and Officer O'Malley did the same. I just shook my head.

She started to grab her crucifix again, and clutched it tightly while she stared at the floor. "There is," she said softly. "But I apparently am not allowed to say anything right now about it."

I felt terrible when she said that. She evidently wanted to get it all off her chest, but I thought that it would be strategically better if she didn't right away. I didn't necessarily want the prosecutor to know what angle we were going for until I got my ducks in a row on this case. I wanted there to be some kind of element of surprise, some way of throwing the prosecutors off their game. That was the only way that I envisioned winning this case.

Officer O'Malley just stared at me for a second. "Okay then, I guess this question and answer session has ended."

"What happens next?"

"I give this file to the prosecutor's office, and they'll decide whether to file charges against you. Your attorney can explain the rest."

At that, Margot and I left Officer O'Malley's office. Slade was waiting for us outside his car, and we got in. "You wanted to know what happens next," I told Margot. "Assuming the prosecutor's office wants to go ahead and charge you, which seems more than likely, given your confession, then you will have to appear before a judge. He'll read you your charges and set a bond for you. Slade will pay that, whatever it is, so you shouldn't spend too much time in jail."

She nodded. "That's okay if I do. I hated being locked up before, of course, but I know that I can survive it. If I can survive seven years in the Pen, I can survive anything. But go on."

"You're familiar with this whole procedure, of course," I said. "But I'll go ahead and tell you anyway, just in case you had forgotten what happens. The next step, after you are read your charges by the judge and given bond is that your case will go to the grand jury. It's a secret proceeding, and, unfortunately, I won't be able to be there. I would expect an indictment, after which you will be formally charged. After that, it's just a matter of getting the case ready for trial. The whole thing is going to hinge on the testimony of the expert witness that I plan to call to the stand."

She didn't say anything, but stared out the window. "I know. You explained all that to me. It just scares me. What happens if the jury doesn't buy my story? And what is going to happen to Slade? He helped me get rid of the body."

"Mom, don't worry about me," Slade said. "I'm sure that I'll be fine. In fact, I plan on coming clean with the prosecutor who will be on my case. I'm going to tell the prosecutor that getting rid of the body, as opposed to going to the authorities, was completely my idea. That doesn't mean that you won't be in trouble, too, but hopefully it will mitigate the damages."

I hoped that Slade was right about that. He faced some serious prison time if things didn't go his way. Obstruction, tampering with evidence, abuse of a corpse...there were so many serious charges that come from doing what they did to Hugh.

Slade grinned. "Hey, maybe I can draw Raphael as my prosecutor again. It would be like old times."

I put my hand on his leg. "I know that you want to make light of this, because that's what you do. But you have to face the fact that what you did was very serious. I hope that you understand that. You might end up serving some time for it." My heart sunk to my shoes as I realized that.

Granted, he wouldn't be serving life in prison. At most, he might serve a few years. I hoped against hope that he was right – that he would somehow beat these charges and perhaps end up with only probation or something along those lines.

"If I do, I do. In the meantime, I better get my publicist on this. Once this shit hits the fan, so soon after the last fiasco, I would imagine the media is going to be all over it." He shook his head. "I can handle whatever happens, though. To me, at least." He closed his eyes briefly and rapidly reopened them. "Oh, sorry, I didn't mean to shut my eyes like that."

"It's okay. Are you okay though?"

I closed my eyes and tuned into his vibrations. Just as I thought, his cheery and chipper demeanor were all for show. He was extremely worried about his mother. I didn't feel that he was worried about his own situation, though. I only felt that he was concerned about Margot.

"I'm fine," he said. "As I told you, don't worry about me. After what I went through in my formative years, I can handle anything at all. Once you've seen your mother shoot your father dead, anything that comes after it is a piece of cake."

We drove along, and ended up at Slade's Malibu home. I let Bella and Gigi out of the SUV and immediately put them into the penned are of Slade's enormous estate. "I'm a little tired," he said. "Too tired to drive all the way back to San Diego. I hope you don't mind if we spend the night here."

"Of course I don't mind," I said. "As you said earlier, you're soon going to be bailing out our firm. I don't think that Harry will want to fire me when the future of the firm is going to be riding on your largesse. I'm sure that I can take off a few days."

I knew that I would have to be back in San Diego soon, though, as I was going to have to pay my respects to Malcolm. A part of me hated to do that, but another part of me, the part that was fond of him before I found out what he did, really wanted to go to his funeral.

We walked into the beautiful home, and I was, once again, struck by the size and beauty of it. The walls of windows, the skylights, the view, the amenities – all of these things were what I marveled at the very first time I saw this place all those months ago. So much had happened since then. It almost seemed like a whirlwind, and it definitely seemed surreal.

Margot went into a downstairs bedroom. She didn't have a change of clothes with her, but Slade explained that he always kept some things for her in this particular room, because occasionally she would come and stay with him throughout the years.

Slade and I went into his enormous bedroom, and I lay down on the bed. Was it really just that morning that I punched Derek at that luncheon and then got really drunk? Again, it seemed like ages ago. One thing was for sure, it had been a really long day. One of the longest days I've had in awhile.

Slade came over to me, lifting up my shirt. "I know that you're very tired," he said. "So I'll try to behave myself, as much as it's completely difficult to do so whenever I'm around you."

I sighed. I wasn't necessarily in the mood, but, as Slade gently rubbed his hands on my breasts and stomach, I started to feel the familiar tingle. "You don't have to behave yourself," I said. "After the day I had today, I feel that this would be a beautiful coda."

He smiled. "That's one of the things I love about you. You can use the word 'coda' properly. I can't say the same about most of the women I've dated."

I laughed. "Just what kind of women have you dated?"

He rolled his eyes. "You know who I've dated. Charlotte, for one. But I've also dated just about every actress and model in Hollywood. None of them ever held my interest like you have, though."

His hand went from my belly and on down to my nether region. As his finger stroked inside of me lightly he whispered, "What do you want tonight, Serena?"

I kissed his lips. "Just vanilla," I said. "I'm so sorry, I'm not…"

"I know," he said. "Neither am I really. But just wait until you see the room I have here. My playroom is one of the most state of the art there is." And then he laughed. "I'm joking, of course. I do have a nice playroom, but it just has standard equipment, really. But sometimes standard equipment can be the best, you know?"

I had to laugh. "I know. Now, shut up and fuck me."

It was his turn to laugh. "I'll get around to it. I just need to feel your soft skin on my fingers just a little bit more." His hand went to my thigh and stroked it as he kissed the back of my neck. "You have to know me by now. I do things in my own time and in my own way."

I wasn't necessarily in the mood for elaborate kink, so I just let the feeling of his skin on mine wash over me. His fingers were making their way up to my breasts, and he pinched the folds of my nipples lightly. The burst of pain that simple act created was exquisite, and I sighed. I rolled over on my back as his legs intertwined with my own. His cock was exposed in all its glory. He lay on top of me, his elbows on either side of my head, as he kissed me slowly. As his fingers touched my arms, I felt the familiar jolt of electricity shoot through me like a lightning bolt. Sometimes I felt the electricity like a gentle wave, and sometimes, like right now, it felt like the earth had opened up and swallowed me whole. I cried out as he maneuvered behind me, his pillowy lips biting and sucking the back of my neck.

I reached behind me and put my hand firmly on his exposed manhood. I gripped it slowly as he groaned. His breath quickened as my stroking became more insistent, firmer and faster. He was behind me, with his hands on my breasts, and I could feel his excitement with my hand. "Slow down," he finally growled. "I need to come, but I want to be inside you when I do."

At that, he rolled me onto my back, and he gently sheathed his manhood and slid it inside of me. I was thoroughly wet and ready to receive him, so the feeling of him being inside of me was that of being complete. I simply couldn't imagine any other place that I would have rather been than right there in that bed with him. His beautiful bed and his beautiful body were combining to wash away every bit of stress that had occurred that day with his mother and with Derek.

I put his head in my hands and looked him right in the eye. And then, without another word, I kissed him. His lips glided gently over mine as his tongue eagerly explored my mouth. I sighed as I felt him stroking in and out of me for what seemed like an eternity. I wanted it to last for an eternity, too.

He lay down beside me and wrapped his right arm around my neck. I took his arm and put it around my waist and held his hand in mine. It was understood by both of us,

I knew, that the love-making wasn't going to make every-thing go away. It couldn't. There was just still so much up in the air, so many things that we were going to have to deal with. Things that I didn't necessarily relish dealing with. Nonetheless, we were able to find comfort in one another, and that felt wonderful.

I cried out as I released my orgasm, and I knew that Slade did as well.

I needed a buffer against the cold, cruel world, and Slade had provided that for me.

I knew, without him even speaking, that I had provided the same thing for him.

Chapter Eight

The next day, it was time to really take action. Slade and I agreed that it was best that Margot turn herself in so that she could get her case moving along. After her interrogation with Officer O'Malley, it was all but inevitable that she was going to be arrested for Hugh's murder. We just decided to be proactive. It was the best thing for us to do, mentally.

I felt awful for Margot, who was sitting in the back of Slade's car, as we drove to the police station. "How do we know charges are going to be filed?" she asked nervously. Her hand was on her crucifix, as she clutched it and zipped it along on its chain back and forth.

"We went through this," Slade said, and we did. "There is no way there won't be charges filed. And, by the way, I…"

We were almost at the police station when we saw them. Throngs of reporters were standing outside the station. There must have been some kind of tipoff that an arrest of Margot was imminent. There also was probably a tipoff that Slade's arrest was imminent as well.

Slade groaned, but by then he had become more than

used to being at the center of a media circus. "I'll handle the reporters," he said to Margot. Then he turned to me. "Do you think we should go ahead and make a statement or just tell them 'no comment,' like we always do?"

I hadn't anticipated that there would be reporters already camped out like they were. I guess I should have seen it coming, after all the media attention that Slade got for his case, but I just didn't. I felt naïve all of a sudden. "Yes, we might as well get up in front of it," I said. "We can possibly control the media narrative before the media narrative controls us. I can't make a statement for you, Slade, of course, since I'm not representing you. You should probably call your own attorney and let him know what's going on."

Slade was already on that. "Hey, Jackson," he said on his phone. "Meet me at the LA police department head-quarters on 1st," he said. "I'll be waiting for you. My car is parked in front of the building on the street."

Slade then nodded at me and got off the phone. "Jackson will be here in a half hour," he said. "His office is five blocks away from here, but he said that he's finishing up an interview with a new client." He took a deep breath. "I don't know why we didn't anticipate this happening. The press is always being tipped off about me."

I looked behind me at Margot. She was sitting in the backseat just staring out the window. "I've never gone through something like this," she said. "They're not all here for me, are they?"

"No, they're probably mainly here for Slade. Slade has been a huge ratings-grabber for the better part of a year now. With the charges being dropped against him in Jordan's case, the media obviously wants to grab onto another scandal involving him." I shook my head. "They're such vultures. I wish that they would, for just one second, imagine what it would be like to be Slade. Hunted. Never left alone. Made to answer for something that he had zero involvement with. Pronounced guilty until proven innocent. The media had been terrible to him the entire time his murder case was active, and I knew that there would be no apologies, either directly to him or on the air to their viewers."

"I know," Margot said. "I was always infuriated by the things that they said about my boy. They always told the viewers that he was guilty, in so many words."

I sucked in some air and blew it out in frustration. Now the media actually had something on Slade. Granted, it was much less salacious than murdering your business partner. And it happened when he was just 18. Regardless, it was a felony, there was no doubt about that. I wondered if the media was going to be just as relentless about this case as they were about Jordan's murder.

In about a half hour, just as Slade said, a man appeared at the door of Slade's car. He was a tall and incredibly hand-some black man with a completely bald head. He was dressed in a very high-dollar suit and sported a Rolex watch on his left wrist. He rapped on the window and Slade put the glass down. "Jackson," he said. "As I called you to tell you, I'm going to be in trouble for what I did with mom's attacker 10 years ago. I'm assuming that those reporters are for me. I need for you to make a statement to them, because we need to get out in front of all of this."

At that, Slade gestured for me to get into the backseat with Margot. Jackson came around and got into the passen-ger's seat. He turned around and grinned at me. "Hello, I'm

Jackson Prejean. I'm Slade's personal attorney. And you are?"

"Serena," I said, shaking his hand. "I was one of the attorney's on Slade's murder case."

"Oh, yes," he said. "I understand that you managed to get that video over to Raphael just in time. At least that's what the media is reporting."

"When did the media start reporting about Slade's case?" I asked.

"It's hitting the papers this morning, and the pundits have been all over it. Everybody is still trying to establish motive for Malcolm doing that. It really has become an even bigger story now that there is a central mystery to be solved. Nobody can quite figure out what happened. Nobody knows why Slade was ready to plead guilty and why he retained the killer as his attorney. I'm sure that there's a piece to this story that everyone isn't getting."

"There is," Slade said. "But I can't tell you about that right now. I can only tell you when the attorney-client privilege will be valid." Since Margot and I were in the car with Slade and Jackson, there wouldn't be attorney-client privilege between the two of them. That privilege would only be valid if there was just the attorney and the client in a closed room when nobody else was around.

"What else is the media reporting?" I asked Jackson.

"Well, the media has been all over Malcolm now. All of his dirty laundry is coming out. His gambling addiction, his ties to the Garancino family, his visits to brothels. All of it."

I hadn't heard about Malcolm visiting brothels, but it fit. "I feel awful for his wife and children," I said. "If this whole murder wasn't tied to Slade, Malcolm's involvement wouldn't even be a thing that the media would have noticed.

Now they're going to have to live with the shame of what Malcolm did, along with grieving his death."

Slade shot me a look, and I knew what he was thinking before he even said it. He was worried that the media, in digging around, would be led to Charlotte somehow. If they did too much poking around, they might establish that connection. If they did, Charlotte would be a loose cannon again. If she had nothing to lose, then she would be absolutely dangerous.

"So, what is your statement going to be to the press?" Slade asked Jackson.

"Since you're not going to try to cover up what you did with your mother's date, then it's just a matter of trying to turn the narrative around to become sympathetic to you. That's going to be difficult, because people are naturally squeamish about people getting rid of corpses. The fact that this guy's disappearance was something that was well-covered by the media when it happened..." He shook his head. "That doesn't work in your favor at all. We're going to have to lay the groundwork for a self-defense claim for Margot, and it starts with this unofficial press conference."

"I understand," Slade said, but he gave me a look, and I knew that he was absolutely worried. I closed my eyes and felt immediately that his worry was more for Margot than for himself. "So, what is your statement going to be?"

"I'm going to get on top of the story. I'm going to tell the media that you were very young when this happened, and that your loyalty to your mother led you to do what you did. I'll explain that you felt that your mother couldn't get a fair trial for Hugh's killing, and that you knew that his homicide was an act of self-defense. I'll explain that all that you wanted was to make sure that your mother didn't spend the rest of her life in prison." He cracked his knuckles, which was a gesture that I was often guilty of myself. "It's all about framing in these cases. If you can frame a crime in a way that makes the defendant look sympathetic, then half the battle is won right there."

I nodded. I knew that was important – framing an issue. If the media framed Slade's involvement as just covering up a murder, then it would be uphill for Slade to get a more positive message out. But if the media went along and framed Slade's crime as simply being the actions of a scared teenager who wanted to protect his mother, then the sentiment would much more be on his side.

"Do you think your framing will work?" I asked Jackson.

"Yes, especially since I have a close contact with the *LA Times*. If we can get the largest paper in Los Angeles to report the story in the way that I want them to, then we'll have a much easier time of it. Most everyone will follow suit."

"What about the 24-hour news channels? They're the ones who incited the media riot around Slade the last time."

"I have some well-placed contacts on all those stations as well. And, I've been a contributor on *CNN* on many different shows. Since that network needs to make sure that I keep fulfilling the terms of my contract, they pretty much will make sure that the story is reported the way I want it to be."

I felt relieved that Slade had a guy like Jackson in his corner. I had always wondered, secretly, just why Malcolm wasn't more like Jackson – coming at the media aggressively, telling Slade's story of innocence. I knew why, now, Malcolm didn't do all those things. I was therefore happy that Slade's story would be out there with this Jackson person.

"Okay, alright," Jackson said with a smile on his face. I

was warming up to this man, for he seemed like a typical happy warrior. He was going to bat for his client, but he was going to do it with aplomb and good humor. That was important. "Let's do this. It's show-time."

At that, we all got out of the car. Somebody from the media spotted us, and the whole throng came at us *en masse*. Before I knew it, we were surrounded by people, cameras, and microphones being shoved in all of our faces.

"Is it true that you're going to be pleading guilty to disposing of a corpse today, Mr. Bridgewell?" somebody asked.

"Do you have any comment on your mother's case?" asked somebody else.

"Why did you dispose of that body?" asked a third person.

"Why did your mother kill Hugh Robbins?" asked yet another person.

Slade took a deep breath. "Please direct all your questions to my counsel, Jackson Prejean," he said, motioning to Jackson. "He'll be my attorney on this case, and he will speak for me. In the meantime, I have to get into the station."

The throng moved towards Jackson, but people continued to shout at me. "Are you the attorney for Ms. Facinelli?" somebody asked. "Do you care to comment on whether or not she is guilty of the murder of Hugh Robbins?"

"I am the attorney for Ms. Facinelli, and I would like to make a statement," I said. "Ms. Facinelli feared for her life and for her safety. Mr. Robbins was illegally in Ms. Facinellis home, and, as you know, her home is considered to be her castle. As such, she has an absolute right to defend herself in her own home if she reasonably felt that she was in danger of death or great bodily harm. She had the right to stand her ground and not retreat."

At that, everybody started talking at once. People were taking pictures of me, with Margot by my side, and I felt threatened myself. Slade came over and put his arm around me protectively. "Everybody get back," he said. "If one of you lays one hand on her, I'll go and get an officer from inside this building to come out here. One question at a time."

"Mr. Bridgewell, is it true that your mother shot Mr. Robbins in cold blood and that she didn't feel threatened for her life at all?"

"No, that's not true. Now, if you will excuse us, we need to see the officers that are presiding over this case. Again, if you have any more questions, please speak with my lawyer, Jackson Prejean."

The media throng didn't seem to be satisfied in the least with this command. They kept pressing and jostling and I felt suffocated. I was getting used to this kind of media attention because of Slade's murder case, but it never quite rose to this level, at least not regarding me. Slade handled it all like a pro, though. He put his arms out, in order to keep everyone back. "We need to go." He looked over at Jackson. "I won't say one word until you get into the room with me, but could you please hold an impromptu press conference out here?"

"Of course," he said with a smile. Then he faced the media throng. "Okay, one question at a time please."

At that, the three of us – Margot, Slade and I – made our way into the building. I looked down at my hands, which were shaking. "Oh my god, I don't think that I've seen anything like that. I mean, I have, but only on television."

"You're lucky then. That kind of thing has been the story of my life, especially lately. But you handled them really well. I'm proud of you."

"Thanks," I said. I still felt shaken, yet, because Slade was right there, by my side, I didn't feel as shaken as I might have.

Slade leaned into me. "I hate to tell you this, but you're going to have to get used to that. Not that those people are interested in my mother, but, since I played a part in this whole thing…" He shook his head. "They're going to be going ape."

"I believe you."

We made our way to Detective O'Malley's office. He stood up when he saw the three of us. "Well, well, well, you just made my job one helluva lot easier. I was going to send the sheriff over to pick up Margot, yet here you guys are."

"Here we are," I said. "Margot would like to turn herself in and start the process."

"Good," he said. "I have already Mirandized you, so I'm going to have to book you into jail. Tomorrow you'll get your first hearing." He looked over at me. "Be in court tomorrow at 9. Her case will be on the docket."

At that, he put the handcuffs on her, and her face looked stricken. I wondered if her mind was tripping back to the days when she was serving prison time for the murder of her husband. As I closed my eyes, I knew that she was thinking about those days. I put my hand on her arm. "You won't serve much time in there. I'll be there at the hearing tomorrow and Slade will post your bond, whatever it is. It's going to be okay."

She nodded, but said nothing at all. She let the officer lead her to the jail, and I went with her as she went through the entire process – being fingerprinted, having her mug

ANNIE JOCOBY

shot taken, being strip-searched. She had to leave all of her valuables in a bag – her watch, her rings, her phone. She convinced them to let her leave her crucifix on, though. "Please," she told him. "I need this. I never take this off, ever."

The guard looked frustrated and shook his head, but he let her keep it. "You can keep that on," he said, "at your own risk. Don't be looking at me if somebody tries to forcibly take that from you."

"Thanks," she said, looking down as he led her into a cell. There were two other ladies in that cell, and they regarded her warily.

"Okay, now, Margot, you know what to do. We'll be seeing you tomorrow in court." I put my hand through the bar and touched her own. "It's going to be okay."

Even as I told her that, though, I was unsure. Was she going to be okay? Could I win this case? It certainly seemed a long-shot. And, if I lost the case, would Slade ever forgive me? I felt so much pressure from all of this. Somehow, I was going to have to pull a rabbit out of the hat. If I didn't, then Slade and Margot's life would be completely upended.

Something like that could spell the end of my fantasy with Slade.

82

Chapter Nine

I went to the lobby of the police station, which was where I was supposed to meet Slade. I nervously looked down at my phone, reading articles about self-defense and pulling up case law on the topic on my *Lexis* account. I knew that the whole thing would hinge on the testimony of the expert witness, but it also would hinge upon which judge I drew for the case. I knew that I could pick the best jury – that was my specialty. I could usually tell when the jurors were lying about something, and that would be my basis for dismissing them.

With the right jury and the right expert, we might stand a chance.

Might.

It seemed like forever before Slade came out with Jackson. "I'm being arrested," he told me. "So go on back to the house."

"Court date tomorrow?"

"Yes. The same courtroom as my mother. We'll both be

out on bail tomorrow, I assume. I know that I will, and hopefully the judge will set a bond for mom."

I had a feeling that was coming. I was going to have to go out and face those reporters all by myself. "I'll see you tomorrow."

He put his arms around me, put his hand in my hair and kissed me passionately. "See you tomorrow."

I left, and, just like I knew would happen, the reporters swarmed me. "Do you have any comment about Mr. Bridgewell's involvement with the murder of Hugh Robbins?" someone asked.

"Do you think that Ms. Facinelli will be getting the death penalty?" shouted another.

"I told you all that I'm going to tell you," I said. "When I gave my impromptu press conference earlier. Now, please stand back and let me get to my car."

They parted and let me walk, but they continued to shout questions at me as I walked to Slade's car. I was going to have to drive his Tesla Model X SUV, which was a car that I had never driven before. I was slightly nervous about that, but I soon got the hang of it, and I drove off to head for Slade's Malibu mansion.

———

When I got to Slade's, I wasn't there five minutes before Harry was calling me. "Serena," he said. "What is going on? Nobody has heard from you since you punched Derek at lunch, although Mr. Bridgewell has called the firm on your behalf."

I didn't want to tell him the truth – that working with Derek turned my stomach. I was going to have to learn how to work with that man, even if it was the very last thing that

I wanted to do. "I apologize, Harry, but I have a new client for us. Margot Facinelli, Mr. Bridgewell's mother."

"Oh, that's a good one. It's been all over the news here because of Mr. Bridgewell's involvement. Poor guy can't catch a break. He's getting his charges dropped for murder, but he's right back into it for this cover-up." He paused for a few seconds. "I suppose you heard the news that Mr. Bridgewell is bailing out our troubled ship? He's retired all of Malcolm's debts and has infused the firm with cash. His people sent over a bill of particulars, and I think that we're going to have to take it. So, your boyfriend is going to be the majority owner of our firm."

"Well, it's a good investment for him."

"It is. Now, do you want to tell me about you and Derek?"

"What about us?"

"You punched him, right at the table in front of everyone. Nobody could understand why you did that."

"I don't want to go into that."

"You don't have to, of course, but I think that you're going to have to learn to work with him. Our firm is very excited to have him, as he has made quite a name for himself in New York City. He's prosecuted a lot of high-profile people there. He's going to be a real asset to us, so please don't mess this up."

I sighed. "I won't mess this up. Now, is there anything else I can do for you?"

"No, but I did want to know when you're coming into the office again."

"The day after tomorrow," I said. "Friday. I have a bond hearing tomorrow for Margot, Slade's mother, and then I'll probably head back to San Diego. I'll be at the funeral, too, of course. It's on Saturday right?"

"Right. I'll see you in a few days then. Are you working remotely?"

"No. I don't have my case files with me."

"Okay, then, I'll see you on Friday."

At that, hung up.

As I walked around the enormous house, I realized that it seemed almost haunted. I remembered when I first got here, how lively it all was. Slade had a charity ball right there in the house, and the charity ball turned into a raucous party afterwards. There were people milling about the house into the next day. Even then, I knew that Slade was trying to escape something. He told me that he enjoyed having people around because it helped him get out of his head.

Now, with nobody around, the enormous place just seemed cavernous. The grand piano had a cover over it, and I looked up at the skylight and saw dust particles streaming. I had assumed that Slade had his cleaning crew up at the house working, even if he couldn't be there on-site, but it looked like nobody had been there for several months.

I went over to the kennel that had the two dogs in it. They were curled up together on their bed, and, when they saw me, they both stretched and yawned and then their little bodies started to gyrate wildly. "Let's go outside," I said, scooping them both up.

I took them to the fenced-in yard and put them down. They explored, sniffing around, before landing on a spot to do their business. They finished and came bounding over to me again.

They followed me into the house, and I gave them both a treat. I sat down on a big chair, and they leaped up on my lap. I pet them absent-mindedly.

Slade called on my phone. "Hey," he said when I picked up. "This is my one phone call. I wanted to let you know that I'm okay. I'm thinking about you."

"I'm thinking about you, too."

"We're going to get out of this."

I knew that Slade wasn't certain of this, even though he certainly tried to sound like he was. "I hope that you're right. This isn't going to be easy, though. Not in the least."

"These cases aren't ever easy, nor are they supposed to be. But I have faith in you. I have faith in Jackson to get me off as well."

"I'll see you tomorrow," I said.

"Yes, tomorrow."

After he hung up, I wandered around the house some more. I also put in a phone call to the expert witness that I needed to call. His name was Dr. Sanderson, and I knew that he specialized in disorders that were associated with trauma. If I could get him to tell the jury that Margot was suffering from acute PTSD, then maybe the jury would acquit her. It would show that she reacted reasonably for a woman in her shoes.

His receptionist answered the phone and told me that he was with a client, but would call me as soon as he could.

When he finally called back, after about an hour, I made an appointment to see him. I wanted to speak with him about what I needed before he met with Margot. I didn't know for a fact that Margot would be granted bail, but I assumed that she would, so I worked with that assumption in mind.

For the rest of the day, I did an endless amount of research on the case. By the time I finally turned in that night, at around 11, I felt like an expert myself on Margot's case. My head was filled with statistics and about how people who suffered from PTSD would react in certain situations. I read case law about Vietnam vets who killed people because they were in the throes of an active PTSD hallucination. I read everything that I needed to read about "Battered Woman's Syndrome." I had to become well-versed on what we needed to prove to the jury to show that Margot was not guilty because she reasonably feared for her life.

I even briefly thought of another defense, temporary insanity, but I felt that Margot probably wouldn't fit that definition. That would require me to show that Margot didn't know the nature of her act at the time of the crime, and, from what Slade told me, that wasn't the case. She clearly knew what she had done.

The other avenue to explore was diminished capacity or a "heat of passion" defense. That would negate the premeditated *mens rea* that would need to be shown by the prosecution to make a murder charge stick. That would mean that Margot could be convicted of manslaughter, as opposed to murder, if I could show diminished capacity or that the killing was done in the "heat of passion." Heat of passion meant that she was so in the grips of her emotions at that time that it caused her to do what she did.

That was going to be Plan B, because if Margot was convicted of manslaughter, she would be back in prison. That wasn't a good choice for anybody, of course, even if her prison sentence was relatively short. Slade wouldn't be happy with that, and Margot...who knew if she would even survive another prison stint? The last one clearly destroyed her. I thought about how she was – so cowering, so afraid, so small. Her body language told me that she was a woman who was beaten down by life. To go to prison when she was in that kind of mental state was just something that I couldn't even contemplate. Nor did I want to.

It was better than her being convicted of murder, of course, but that wasn't saying much.

By the time I finally went to sleep, I was confident that I had done enough preliminary research. It didn't reassure me, necessarily, because I still foresaw an uphill battle in trying to convince the jury that Margot reasonably feared for her life. But, I at least felt that I had somewhat of a grip on what was going to happen.

Chapter Ten

Slade made bail the next day. I went to the courthouse to pick him up and appear in court for Margot, after being jostled by the reporters yet again. Slade was first, as he greeted me outside the courthouse. "I'm free," he said, with Jackson right behind him. "The judge only made my bond $50,000, which is a good sign. I'm guessing that he's not necessarily thinking that my crime is all that serious."

I nodded my head. "That really is a good sign. That bond amount wasn't much."

He hugged me, and I felt my head against his hard pecs. "I missed you last night," he said. "I was in my jail cell, and all that I could think about was you."

I smiled. "I felt the same way." I sighed. "But I'm just a tad nervous over Margot's hearing. I hope that the judge gives her bail. He might not, though. After all, she sorta ran after she killed Hugh by going to New York City. That doesn't look good, and it also doesn't look good that you have a private plane and a house in Italy for her to go. I'm sure that the prosecutor is aware of all of these factors. Just fair warning."

"I know. Good luck anyhow. I don't want to put any pressure on you about this, at least any more pressure than I have to."

"Don't worry. Well, I need to go to her courtroom and do what I can."

I walked down the hall to Margot's courtroom. I was on the docket, but I was first, so, when Margot was brought in, I knew that we would be getting out of there soon. I approached the bench, and the judge read her charges. "Margot Facinelli, you've been charged by the State of California with one count of first degree murder. How do you plead?"

She looked at me with wide eyes. "Not guilty you're honor."

The judge looked at the prosecutor. "Do you have any objections to my setting bond for Ms. Facinelli?" He looked over at me, smiled, and looked back at the prosecutor. "Bear in mind that Ms. Facinelli can surely make any bail I set for her, seeing that her son can buy half of the State of California, with money left over."

The other attorneys and observers in the court laughed when the judge said this, and I got a chuckle out of it as well. "No, your honor," the prosecutor said. "There's nothing in her background that would make her a flight risk."

I felt a bit surprised about that, considering that Margot actually did flee to New York City after she killed Hugh, but, of course, I kept my mouth shut. "Okay, then, bail is set for $10 million." He banged the gavel, and I left the bench with Margot.

"What's next?" she asked me.

"Slade posts your bond and you go home."

She took my hand and squeezed it. "Thank you."

"Of course."

I got out into the hallway, and Slade was waiting for me. "I guess she got a bond?"

"Yeah. $10 million, which seems a bit excessive."

He shrugged his shoulders. "Not a big deal. I'll call my accountant and have him pay the bond." He shook his head. "Thank god I got Phil, my accountant, to release all my assets and cash from the trust I constructed when I thought I was going to prison." He then got on his phone and called his accountant while I sat next to him.

"Okay," he said, getting off the phone. "It's all set. Now, let's get back to my home. I think that you and I have some catching up to do, if you know what I mean."

I did know what he meant, as he had hinted around about his playroom. He said that he had standard equipment in there, so I wasn't necessarily expecting anything grand, but I was looking forward to it all the same.

I was still worried about his mother, of course, but that particular stressor was just going to have to wait. There wasn't much that could be done about it right at that moment anyhow.

We drove back to his house, and he led me straight back to a locked door. With a turn of a key, I was inside. I was impressed with what I saw inside, but he was right - there wasn't anything that was out of the ordinary. It was just a beautiful room, much more beautiful than other dungeons I had seen in my time in New York City. The walls were red, of course, as they usually were, but, in the middle of the room was a beautiful bed with four posters and a canopy-like top overhead. On one of the walls was a St. Andrew's Cross, and there was a spanking bench, and handcuffs on the walls. In the corner of the room, peculiarly, was a baby grand piano, much like what he had in one of his rooms upstairs.

He raised his eyebrow. "I don't think that I've sufficiently punished you for what you did in getting that videotape without my knowledge," he said. "I think that it's way overdue."

"I couldn't agree more," I said. "I did go against your wishes, and I think that I need to take whatever you have to give."

I felt completely excited as he unzipped my skirt and unbuttoned my blouse. He turned to my bra and flicked it off with one finger. He looked down at my feet. "Those shoes can stay," he said, pointing to my red high-heeled Christian Louboutin shoes. "But the hose have to go."

He gently pushed me down on a plush red chair and raised my legs. He slowly and sensuously rolled my panty hose down from my waist, inch by inch. With every millimeter he rolled down my hose, he covered that area with little nibbles, licks and kisses. He rolled down my hose to my thighs, and he licked, caressed and nibbled the area that was previously covered by the hose. Then down to my knees, and did the same. Down to my calves, and, finally, they were off. My legs were covered with his gentle mouth all the way down. This felt amazing, so amazing that I tried to contain my orgasm. I knew that, since we were in play mode, he was going to force me to contain my release, so I was going to have to have some self-control with it.

Next was my panties. He made his way back up my legs, leaving trails of kisses, sucks and nibbles which burned my skin completely. His deft fingers tugged on my panties as I leaned back in the chair. I wrapped my legs around his back, and he slowly rolled my underwear off of me. He returned to the area, his mouth and tongue teasing my inner folds and clit. I once again tried to contain myself, but it was no use. I had my first ecstatic release of the evening, and Slade looked at me. "You're going to pay for that," he said. "You have to control your orgasms until the very end of this." Then he put my high heels back on my feet. "Those shoes are sexy," he said. "So I'd like you keep them on."

I nodded my head, knowing that it was going to be impossible to do as Slade was ordering me to. Then, when he picked me up and bent me over the spanking bench, securing my hands with the handcuffs that were attached to the underside of the bench, I knew that I was going to have problems containing myself. Once again, I was helpless as I couldn't move, and I had no idea what was coming. But Slade apparently was determined that I wasn't going to be able to cry out, because he put the ball gag over my mouth.

I was on this bench, my wrists firmly secured to the bench, my head dangling down. The anticipation on what was going to happen was killing me. Slade was deliberately quiet, and I knew that this was part of his game - he was going to tease me by making me sweat, not knowing when he was going to strike or what he was going to do. My adrenaline was going haywire by this point, and every single synapse in my body was on high alert. There was absolute silence in the room for the longest time, but then I heard music playing. It was a Beethoven piece and it sounded like it was live.

I looked over and Slade was sitting at the grand piano. I swallowed hard, wondering when he was going to come over and give me my punishment for defying me, and realized that this was all part of his game. I was starting to feel uncomfortable in this position, and I craved for him to come over and attend to me. Still, he sat at the piano and his fingers were pounding the keys feverishly. I had to admit that I was impressed by his talent on the instrument, for it seemed like he was classically trained. He started to hit his crescendo, his eyes closed, and his breathing coming hard.

Then he looked at me and realized that I was staring at him and he smiled. He came over and put a blindfold over my eyes and I heard him starting to play the piano again. I knew that was his way of controlling what was going to happen, and I had to admit, after he out the blindfold over me, everything became much more intense. He started another dramatic piano piece, one that I recognized as being by Tchaikovsky. I didn't know the exact piece, but I did know the different flourishes that were signature to all the great composers, and it was unmistakable that this particular piece was by the Russian composer.

It was almost agonizing for me to be in that position, with no idea whatsoever when he was going to come back over to me. I lifted my head, because in the position that it was in, all the blood was rushing to it and it was starting to give me a blinding headache. I swallowed hard, but I had to admit that waiting there, while Slade played this exquisite and complex piano piece, was extremely difficult.

He finally finished this piece, and that made the anticipation heighten again. I, once again, started to feel anxious about what was going to happen and when. All this waiting was becoming more and more agonizing for me, but, I had to admit, it also was getting my juices flowing. My adrenaline was heightened by the fact that Slade had stopped playing the piano, yet he still wasn't going anything. He knew just what he was doing in making me wait, because it was truly becoming excruciating.

He must have been walking around silent as a cat, because I never heard him come up behind me. But he apparently did, so, when the paddle thwacked my buttocks, it was a huge surprise and this caused the sensation to drive me absolutely wild. The pain that this whack was causing me was nothing compared to the psychological torture that followed, because, after he whacked me that one time, I didn't feel anything again for several minutes. These minutes, however, felt like hours, as time seemed to stand completely still.

He was teasing me as a cat might tease a mouse. I had never before experienced such a psychological rush as I did while I stood over that bench with the blindfold over my eyes. I tried to control my breathing, because I found myself almost hyperventilating.

I finally felt him spread my legs and secure them to the floor. I desperately hoped that this was a precursor to what he was going to do, and I wasn't disappointed. I felt the whack of his paddle three times in rapid succession, each time stung worse than the last. He wasn't going easy, as he was putting all his might every time the paddle hit my bare buttocks. The sting of the wood brought tears to my eyes, although I wasn't quite sure if these tears were from plea-sure or pain.

Then, just like that, it was over. He unhooked my feet from the bottom of the bench, my hands from the top, and took off the blindfold. My legs felt unsteady as he removed the ball-gag and looked me right in the eye. "There it is," he said. "Don't go against my wishes again."

I nodded my head weakly. I had to admit, his toying with me before he paddled me was more torturous than the actual pain of the wood. It was also something that I had never before experienced. I didn't tell him that I would never disobey him, though, because I knew that I would be lying. I would take the punishment every time, however, and I loved taking it. It was exhilarating.

"Come here," he said, leading me over to the bed. He put my blindfold back on me and turned me around so that my stomach was on the bed. He put some soothing balm on my buttocks, and the cooling feeling was a great relief because it took away most of the sting. Then he started to massage my back, which also felt great, because, in my position over that spanking bench, my back was starting to kink up, causing me a great deal of pain. He was softly singing a song while he rubbed my back, and, while I didn't recognize the song, I loved it.

He soon was kissing my back, and I could feel his manhood right near my inner folds. I sighed as I waited for him to enter me. I wriggled around on the bed, wanting to feel his soft skin against mine. I needed for the heat of his body to meld with mine. I was craving that.

He continued to tease me, as his commanding and strong hands moved from my back to my thighs and calves. With circular motions, he made his way down, and I knew that this was another way that he was trying to torture me. It was almost painful to me not to have him inside of me. My clit felt like it was on fire, and I wanted to touch myself because I was so turned on by what he was doing.

I finally realized what I was craving, as his manhood slowly entered me. The fire inside me grew from the embers to a raging inferno, and I cried out in ecstasy. "Holy hell!" I cried as I bucked up on the bed. My orgasm started the second he entered me, and it spread throughout my body like a conflagration that was out of control.

He flipped me around, sat down on the bed and picked me up. He lowered me down on his hard cock, and he rooted deeply inside me. His lips found mine with an urgency that made me come hard again. He thrust into me again and again, and I threw back my head and screamed out loud.

"God, Serena, you feel so amazing," he said as he stroked in and out of me with a sense of urgency that bordered on desperation.

I had no words for what I was feeling. It was that powerful. All that I knew was that I had to always have him with me. If I didn't, I would be absolutely devastated. Absolutely devastated.

After some length of time, which seemed like hours, he finally had his own release. He breathed hard as he kissed me and lay me back down on the bed. His hands went through my hair as his tender mouth found my own again and again. I groaned, feeling completely and totally sated.

He smiled. "Let's go upstairs to my bedroom, and we'll continue this."

I nodded, again at a loss for words.

At that, he picked me up in his strong arms and I realized that he had an elevator. That was something that I hadn't noticed before, as it was somewhat hidden in the corner. We rode the elevator to his bedroom level and he carried me to his bedroom and lay me down on his bed.

He lay next to me, and stroked my body until he was hard again. As I felt his manhood enter me again, I knew that my life was complete. I had to live for every passing moment, because these moments were all that we had. Until he committed to me and to our future, we only had moments.

I hoped and prayed that we could always be together, but, in the back of my mind, I definitely had my doubts.

Chapter Eleven

The next day, we went to the jail to pick up Margot. The poor woman looked like she was beaten down. She was a slight woman anyhow, and it seemed as if she had shrunk even more after her experience in jail. My heart broke, because I knew that Slade's heart was breaking. I could see it in his eyes as he watched her frail frame coming towards our car, and, when I closed my eyes to tune into his vibrations, I felt the infinite sadness that was roiling throughout his soul.

We walked back to Slade's SUV, Margot walking slowly. "Oh, come mom, it wasn't as bad as all that," Slade said, doing his usual habit of trying to make light of serious situations. "I know that you got a gourmet meal in there."

She shook her head. "I can't go back to that," she said with a small voice. "You're right, being in jail for a night wasn't that bad, and thank you for bailing me out. But I can't go back to that."

I closed my eyes and tried hard to tune into her vibrations to see how stressed she was. And, what I picked up on alarmed me. I felt that she was grieving because she didn't believe that she would beat this charge, but I also felt something else.

I felt that she was literally going to kill herself if she had to go back to prison. I could feel that as strongly as I had felt anything in my life.

Slade was still trying to cheer her up with jokes, but it was clear that she wasn't having it.

"Oh, come on, what more could you ask for? You get three hots and a cot, and all the free time you could possibly ask for." He smiled at his mother, but, when he looked at me, the worry in his eyes was palpable. I didn't even have to try to tune into his vibrations to know that he was as devastated as his mother upon seeing her.

I put my arm around him. He needed my support more than ever at that moment. My touch seemed to be just what he needed, because he stopped trying to make dumb jokes and got quiet.

I then went over to Margot and put my arm around her. She seemed to crumple, and she put her face on my shoulder and started to cry.

Slade looked over at her, and shook his head. I knew that Margot was tearing him up inside, but as always, he worked hard not to show it. He went to his SUV without a word, and I got in with Margot in the back.

That night, we ate dinner in an uncomfortable silence. None of us had words, because all of us were fearing the worst for her.

Especially me.

The next morning, I knew that I had to have a talk with Slade. I woke up next to him, and found him lying there, just watching me with a longing expression on his beautiful face. "I found a new San Diego house for my mom to live in," he said. "She'll be moving in tomorrow. I know that we need our alone time." He nuzzled me. "Don't you agree?"

"I couldn't agree more."

He kissed me and I reveled in the way his lips were slowly and sensuously gliding over my own. "Slade, we better go," I said. "We need to get to the office so that I can start preparing your mother's case."

But Slade had other ideas. He continued to kiss me, and I felt myself melting into him. I reared back my head as his tongue circled my nipples and his hands roamed down my stomach and onto my nether-regions. His finger entered me, and his manhood was rock-hard. I could feel him just outside my opening. I spread my legs eagerly, and Slade put two of his fingers inside of me. He then picked me up and carried me across the room. He sat down in his chair and straddled my legs across his lap.

He put his hands on my back, and lightly ran them across it. I felt the tingles on my skin as his gentle touch soothed me. I felt cleansed by the way he was stroking me. He wrapped his arms tightly around me and rocked into me slowly and deliberately. I groaned as I felt his manhood fill me up. He stroked in and out for what seemed like an eternity, while his gentle lips glided skillfully over my own.

I felt him come inside of me, and I had my sweet release at the same time. We usually used condoms, but we didn't this morning, and that was okay. I had started taking birth control pills, so, even though I was nervous because I hadn't gone through an entire cycle yet, I thought that the odds were in our favor. He kissed me some more, and I moved off of him. "That was amazing, as usual, but we really do have to get going."

"Always the scold," Slade teased. "But you're right. I'd love just to stay right here with you all day long, but we have things to do and things to discuss."

"Like Charlotte. We need to discuss her."

Slade shook his head. "I don't know what's up her sleeve. I think, and don't quote me on this, but I think that I have her cowed. But with her, you just never know. All that I know is that I'm in a really bad position with her, because I don't know what will happen if she finally gets a wild hair and decides that she doesn't really care, after all, about the fate of her own career. If she ever decides that, then she'll be dangerous indeed."

"Why do you think that she'll get to that point?"

"I think that she's contained, but then again, how can you contain somebody who is literally crazy?"

"That's the age-old question, isn't it?"

"Always. Anyhow, that's where we left it."

Slade picked up on my reticence, because, after a few minutes, he put his arms around me. "There's something you're not telling me."

"Yes." I took a deep breath. I hadn't actually talked to Margot, but I knew what she was planning. Still, I was going to tell him a white lie, because he would never believe it if I told him that I picked up on Margot's vibrations and knew what was going on. "Margot talked to me yesterday. She said some things that concern me greatly."

Slade looked worried. "What sort of things?"

I went over to the bed and sat on it, and I pat the seat next to me. Slade came over and sat down. He looked worried, and I felt just as worried. "She implied to me that she might kill herself before she goes back to prison again.

If she's found guilty, she might not make it to prison. She knows that if she's convicted, she probably wouldn't ever see the outside of a prison cell again. So, if I lose this case, I'm really afraid that she's going to do something drastic."

Slade nodded his head and looked at the wall. His hands were clasped in front of him as he just stared. "I was afraid of that," he said softly. "Mom was changed so much from her last prison term. She went into prison a loud, fun and lively woman. She loved to cook and she loved to paint and sing. She was very young, you have to remember, when she went to prison. She had me when she was only 15, and she was 22 when she killed my father. It was hard for her to be behind bars for all those years. Especially since I was never allowed to visit her." He shook his head. "Damn Helen for keeping me away from her all those years." He got quiet as he looked at the wall some more. "Damn her. Anyhow, when my mom got out, she was a different person than what I remembered. That was why it was so important to me to keep Charlotte in check all those years."

"I understand it was hard for you," I said, putting my arm around Slade. "And for your mom."

"Yes," Slade said, but I could tell that he wasn't really into talking about this situation anymore. "Well, do what you can do," he said lightly. I knew that his wall was up, his emotional wall that held back all the tragic things that had happened in his life. Slade was a master at covering up what he was really feeling. I've known that from the start, which was why I was forever grateful for those moments when he became vulnerable to me. Those moments meant the world to me.

"So, I guess I need to get to work on Margot's case," I said. "And I have to eventually get back to San Diego. I do need to go to Malcolm's funeral, even if that's the last place I want to be."

"I need to go into my office today, so it's just as well that we stay here for awhile. I need to speak with my team about my transitioning back to full-time soon. After all this bullshit is over, I'm going to get back to it, and, I have to say, I can't wait."

Later on that day, after Slade called the movers for his mother's new home in San Diego, and preparations were made to move her into the home, I got in contact with Dr. Sanderson. I didn't go into the office, preferring to work from home. I wasn't quite ready to be in the presence of Derek again. To my relief, Dr. Sanderson had an opening for me to talk with him and brief him on Margot's case. I wanted to pick his brain and see if this was a case that seemed to be one that we had a chance on, and then I wanted him to actually evaluate Margot.

I parted ways with Slade that morning, as he went into the office to have his meeting with his team. He was going to be going back in the near future, and the company wanted to make that happen as soon as possible.

I still felt vaguely uncomfortable about all of that and about my future with him. I constantly felt slightly off-balance with Slade, and it was a feeling that I hated. He was going to return to live in LA, at this house, and he refused to discuss what was going to happen with us if he did so. I wanted to take the bull by the horns and just force him to tell me what he thought was going to happen with us, but I couldn't bring myself to.

So, I ended up not talking to him about that, again, and

went about my business. I was an independent woman, goddammit, and I didn't need a man to validate me. Not even a man like Slade. I loved him deeply. I probably loved him more deeply than I had ever allowed myself to love anyone, and there would be an irrevocable hole that would be left in my heart if we ever broke up. But I had to put that feeling aside and simply take things as they came.

I got to Dr. Sanderson's office at 10 AM. It was a beautiful office downtown in one of the high-rises, and it was right down the street from my own office. When I arrived, I didn't have to wait. The receptionist, Dawn, explained to me that Dr. Sanderson was waiting for me and that I could go on back.

"Thank you," I said, as she led me behind the door and down the corridor to Dr. Sanderson's office. It was a gorgeous office with wood paneling and a mahogany desk. The lighting was soft, and the carpet in the office was plush and new. It even had a new-carpet smell.

Dr. Sanderson stood up when I went through the door. "Hello, Ms. Roberts," he said to me, extending his hand. "It's so good to see you again."

"And you," I said, taking a seat on the leather couch that was at the outer-edge of his office.

"I understand you have a case for me to evaluate," he said, getting out his pen and paper. "Tell me about that."

"Her name is Margot. She's 43 years old and she has a checkered history, to say the very least." I then told Dr. Sanderson all about her – about her abusive marriage, her stint in prison, her rapes by prison guards, and how that all led into her shooting Hugh. The doctor listened carefully, while he made copious notes.

When I finally finished telling Dr. Sanderson the basics about his future client, he was quiet for a few minutes. He made a bridge with his hands as he appeared to contemplate what I had just told him. He finally just took a deep breath and blew it out. "I'll evaluate her. I was just thinking that I've had a similar case as this. I gave expert testimony on Battered Wife Syndrome and PTSD. It was one of the most difficult cases of my career, unfortunately."

"Why was that?"

"Well, of course, in the case of Battered Wife Syndrome, the direction of the violence is from the abused to the abuser. The classic case is where a woman, or a man, kills his or her partner after years of physical and/or mental abuse. It's a difficult defense, even if that is the case. My other case, the one that was like yours, was eerily similar. It was a woman who was abused by multiple men in her life, and she killed somebody who she felt had threatened her. She was in the throes of flashbacks when she did it."

"Was that case successful?"

"Unfortunately, no, it wasn't. Well, that's not entirely true. She was charged with first-degree murder, but was convicted of manslaughter. So, it was a partial victory."

I picked up a paper weight on his desk. It was an absent-minded thing that I tended to do when I was feeling stressed. This doctor wasn't giving me confidence that Margot's case was winnable.

"I know what you're thinking," he said. "But that other case wasn't the same as this case. Your client has the added stressor of having been in prison after killing her prior abuser, and being re-victimized while she was there. That could very well tip the jury in her favor. I'll be honest, though, it's a long-shot."

"A long-shot, but not impossible, right?"

"Not impossible. Nothing is ever impossible. I need to see her right away, though, and evaluate her. When can she come in?"

"Anytime. She doesn't work. She's moving into a new home today, but, other than that, I think that she should be free."

"Make an appointment with my receptionist on your way out. I'll evaluate her and then I'll give you my honest opinion on whether or not I can do justice for your client."

"Thank you. That's all that I can really ask."

I shook his hand, and stood up to leave.

"Thank you for considering me again," he said. "I have enjoyed working with you in the past, and I hope that we can be successful with this case." He was referring to the fact that I had secured him for another case that our legal team actually won.

I hoped and prayed this case would be just as successful.

After I left Dr. Sanderson's office, I felt slightly emboldened. I went across the street to a deli and got a veggie sandwich and I realized that I was just running and avoiding. It was human nature to run and avoid difficult situations, so I wasn't beating myself up about that, exactly. What I was doing, however, was thinking about how I could beat the demons that Derek represented in my life. Could I confront him and stand up to him? Could I show him that I wasn't afraid of him? Could I convince him, and myself, that he didn't beat me?

I didn't know, but I was going to find out soon. I was going to have to see him at Malcolm's funeral, and then I was going to have to go back to my own home. I had to be strong and face my fears about him. I couldn't give him power over my life. I refused to give him this power. I saw what happened when you give up your power – you end up like Margot, beaten down by the world. I didn't want the same thing to happen to me.

It wasn't going to happen to me.

When I got back to Slade's LA home, I found him and we packed up to go back to San Diego. I was nervous, so nervous about the fact that I was going to be seeing everyone from my office and was going to have to face them. Nervous about seeing Derek.

"Don't worry," Slade said, putting his arm around me. He seemed to read my mind. "It's going to be okay."

"The funeral is tomorrow. It's going to be a huge affair, I would imagine. Malcolm knew a lot of people."

"But that's not what you're worried about." He punched me lightly on the arm. "Who knows? Maybe that bastard won't be there at the church. After all, he didn't know Malcolm at all. Why would be pay his respects to someone that he didn't know?"

I had to admit, Slade had a point. I shrugged my shoulders. "I don't know. What I do know is that he's an ass-kisser. He always was in school, anyhow. He'll probably go just to save face with his new co-workers." I tried to make light of the situation, as Slade always tried to with every serious situation. "And he'll probably be there just to torment me."

We made our way to Slade's SUV, and packed it up, along with the two dogs, who were eager to get into their carrier. They associated their carrier with going someplace new, so they usually were excited by the prospect of traveling in the car. Our plan was to go back to Slade's house, spend the night, and go to the funeral in the morning.

The next day, I dressed in a black dress and Slade put on a dark suit. He sighed. "I hope that the media isn't going to be there," he said. "I don't want to mess with that today."

"One would think that they would be respectful, but, then again, they've never been respectful to you the entire time your case was going. Why would they start today?"

"You're right about that."

He held my hand and we made our way to his Tesla after I put Bella and Gigi out in the backyard. They were getting so big and they entertained me so much. Nothing gave me joy like watching their two little fat bodies running after a lizard or chasing each other around. Of course, being with Slade also gave me immense joy, so I had to count my blessings. I had to think of these happy thoughts for when I eventually had to face Derek.

We got to the church, and, just like I feared, Derek was standing out in front with some of my other co-workers, including the repulsive Cindy. And, just like Slade had feared, the media was out in force. Malcolm's death was at the center of this huge story about Jordan's death. When it was revealed that he did it, the media frenzy went into overdrive.

As we approached the church, St. Paul's Episcopal, which was a large traditional church downtown, there was a buzz amongst the reporters who were camped out just beyond the church property. I felt sick. These people were such vultures. How dare they show up to a man's funeral? In fact, they weren't just there to take pictures of Slade, they had news teams camped out front as well. I saw several men and women with microphones and cameras trained on them. They weren't on the church property, of course, as they weren't allowed. They therefore had to give us a wide berth, but, when Slade and I approached the front door of the church, they immediately started shouting to him to make a comment.

Slade just shook his head and ushered me into the heavy wooden doors of the church.

I went up to the casket, and looked in. I immediately thought about my mother. I didn't go to her funeral, because I just couldn't handle it. I told my family that I was getting my nails done, because I was covering up my true feelings. I really went to the woods that day and tried to forget about the fact that I had lost my mother in the most devastating way possible. Even the fact that the media was here at Malcolm's funeral brought me back to my mother's death, because the media was all over my family for awhile as well. After all, the McDonald's massacre was huge news, and my mother was the last person killed. They didn't leave my poor father alone. I hated them for that, and I hated them for being at this funeral.

Malcolm looked peaceful, surprisingly enough. There wasn't any reason for a closed-casket thing, as he had hanged himself. Well, he was hanged. Whether or not he did it was another matter.

Slade was right behind me, and, when I turned around, I saw the widow and the three girls in the front pew. My heart went out to them. How must his poor widow feel, knowing that her husband did all that he did? Did she have any inkling that he was living a double life, or was she completely blind-sided? Was she being harassed by the media night and day?

I closed my eyes and concentrated on her. I seemed to get my answer to my questions. She was heartbroken, absolutely heartbroken. It showed on her face, as she had all the tell-tale signs that she hadn't gotten much sleep in the past few days. She had bags under her eyes that she had tried to cover up with makeup, and she was very pale. She hung her head and her shoulders slumped. A daughter was on either side of her, and she was gripping their hands tightly. They were very young, less than 10, and they were crying.

My heart went out to all of them. It made me sick that they were yet more victims of Charlotte's craziness. What other innocent people were going to be devastated because of that woman? Jane, Margot, Malcolm's widow and children, me...not to mention Slade. So many devastated people and all because of one psychotic bitch who needed to be put in her place.

I went up to her and I kneeled down and put my hand on her shoulder. I tried to communicate to her without a word that she wasn't alone. She nodded her head and tried to hold back more tears. "Thank you," she said. She seemed to understand what I was trying to convey, and that heartened me.

I stood up and Slade was waiting for me. We took our seats in our pew and, after about another half hour of people proceeding past the casket, the minister started his sermon.

While the minister was speaking, I kept looking over at Slade. He was an atheist – was he thinking that this guy was full of it? After all, the sermon was all about God's love and grace. I closed my eyes and Slade didn't seem to be cynical about it. He was listening intently and didn't seem to be bored. For some reason, this made me love him all the more. He showed that he could be respectful when he really needed to, even when he was presented with situations that should have made him feel uncomfortable.

I felt some tears coming to my eyes. I was surprised how affecting this sermon was. Maybe it was the words that the minister was speaking, maybe it was the fact that I really was mourning Malcolm more than I acknowledged to myself, or maybe it was that everything was still so chaotic in my life. Probably a combination of all of these things were making me feel devastated. Slade noticed my tears and he put his arm around me while he listened to the minister speaking.

He gripped my hand tightly, and I felt comforted.

The service was over after about an hour of the minister speaking, and I wanted to get out of there. It was a touching sermon, but I didn't want to face my co-workers, especially Derek. Slade and I high-tailed it out of there, as opposed to standing around and talking with everyone. We also didn't go to the reception that was happening afterwards. I just wasn't mentally ready for any of that, and I didn't want to face questions about my punching Derek just yet. I thought that I would just be a distraction anyhow. We therefore left right away, after ignoring the reporters who were still camped just outside of the church property.

On the way back to Slade's home, he took my hand. "That was a nice service," he said.

"It was. Did it make you uncomfortable at all?"

He shook his head. "No. I mean, I don't believe in all of that, of course, but I know that people take comfort in their beliefs, so I think that these services provide something good for the survivors of tragedy."

We were quiet for a little while as I watched out the window and Slade concentrated on the road. I eventually decided to bring up a delicate issue, although I was apprehensive about doing so. "Did you go to your father's funeral?"

Slade took a deep breath. "No. I was only 7, but that was when I decided that there wasn't a God. I used to say my prayers every single evening, and I always prayed that my father would stop beating my mother. Nobody ever heard me. Then, when my mother went to prison, I knew that there wasn't anybody listening to me. How could there be when that was the outcome?"

I had to admit that he made a lot of sense. "So you didn't go to the funeral because you felt that it would be a sham?"

"Yeah. Even at that age, I knew that it would be a sham. Besides, I was happy that my father was dead. I didn't want to pay my respects, so to speak. I told the social worker who was assigned to my case in foster care that I refused to go to that funeral, and, to her credit, she didn't force me to. So, I haven't ever been to a funeral until just now."

All at once, I saw behind his façade. Slade had such a careful armor around him that it was difficult for me, a natural empath, to really understand what was underneath. He had so many carefully constructed walls that made sure that he never really absorbed negative feelings. I now knew that, underneath it all, he was still that scared little boy who was angry with the world. He probably learned to stuff down his feelings when he was in foster care and, especially, when he lived with the icy Helen. It was a wonder that he was as well-adjusted as he was.

I took his hand and kissed it. He smiled at me, but he couldn't hide the small tears that had formed in the corner of his eyes. I ran my fingers through his hair and he shook his head. "I didn't think that I would have been affected like that," he said. "I didn't realize that going to a funeral of a slimeball would be so moving."

"Sometimes things can surprise you," I said. "For reasons that you didn't expect."

He nodded his head, and said nothing more.

We drove to his house in silence.

Chapter Twelve

The next day, I went into work. I knew that chances were the Derek would be there, and I had to go ahead and face it sooner or later, so I decided just to bite the bullet and do it. Being at Malcolm's funeral kind of prepared me for being around my co-workers, especially Derek, and it was time to really get back to being immersed in the office culture. Cindy, of course, was the first person into my office. "We missed you," she said to me. "Where have you been? Everybody has been talking about you and Derek. Why did you punch him like that?"

I cleared my throat. I wasn't about to tell this parasite the real reason why I would do something like that, of course. "I lost my head. Listen, I need to schedule some depositions on this new case we have. Can you get Anita to reserve the court reporter and the conference room for me?"

She rolled her eyes. "I think you can do that yourself." She sat there just looking at me, and I knew that she wasn't about to let the Derek thing go. "Now, tell me again why you would punch Derek like that? He's a brand-new hire, and we can't lose him. He came very highly recommended."

I tried to deflect, but I knew she wasn't going to be happy until I told her everything. "I'll tell you later, but, truly, I've been gone from the office for a few days and I have a shit-ton of work to do. We have a new case. Margot Facinelli. I have to work my ass off on this case if I am going to have any chance of winning."

"I know that case. Slade's mother." She shook her head. "From the frying pan to the fire, I say. The media was all over Slade's case and they're really all over this one too. I hear Slade helped her get rid of the body. After his murder charge went away, the media was disappointed that he didn't go to the hoosegow. Now they know that they have him, and they're really salivating."

"Yes," I said, looking down at one of my files. "I understand all of that. I can't speak for Slade and what happened there. As you know, he has another attorney defending him, Jackson Prejean. He's a celebrity attorney, so he knows the ropes. He's not our concern anymore. Margot is. Hopefully the media won't be interested in her as much as they are in him."

"Ironic, considering she was the one who killed a man." She twirled one blonde lock around her finger nervously. "She's the one who did the killing and he's the one who the media is obsessed with again." She lowered her voice. "I guess the media loves him because he's so camera-ready. If he was only half as good-looking, I doubt that he would get all this attention all the time. Being gorgeous is a curse sometimes. I know from experience." She smirked, so I knew that she wasn't trying to make a joke. She really had a high opinion of herself. She might have been kinda cute, but I didn't think that she was as hot as she thought she was.

"Well, I wouldn't know about that."

"Right." She leaned back in her chair. "You're not chopped liver yourself you know."

I groaned. I didn't want to keep talking to her, yet she made no moves towards the door. "Listen, I would love to keep on chatting with you, but I really have to get with Anita about scheduling those depositions. I also have to get Margot in to be evaluated by Dr. Sanderson. I hope to get this to trial by the end of the year so that we can get all of this behind us. So..." I gestured towards the door while I looked at it.

"I get the hint," she said.

Finally.

"I get the hint, but this conversation is only tabled. I really need to know why you would punch Derek in the nose the way that you did, right in front of everyone. I mean, you just met the guy, right?"

I took a deep breath, hoping that this nosy bitch couldn't figure out what was really going on in my head. "Right."

She got up to leave, but then she sat right back down. "Wait. You're from the East Coast, aren't you? I mean, I know that you're also a transplant from New York, but aren't you originally from Maine?"

I felt the icy fear creeping up in my veins as she sat there looking at me. I could see her wheels turning. I bowed my head and started to play with my paper-weight. That was one of the things that I tended to do whenever I was nervous, and I didn't want her to see how nervous I really was. "Yes. I'm from an..."

"Unincorporated town outside of Portland," she said.

"You must have known Derek when you were in high school. That's where he's from, too. He's your same age as well."

I sighed. There wasn't going to be any hiding the fact that I knew Derek from before. Not when Cindy knew the truth. "Yes, I knew him. Now, please, I have to get to work."

"What happened? Was he a bully? Was he mean to you? I know that he was some kind of popular jock type. Did you run in the same circles?"

"No." I looked desperately towards the door, hoping that somebody would come and save me from this third degree I was getting from Cindy. "We didn't run in the same circles at all. I was more of a Goth kid. I went to raves and certainly didn't run with the same kinds of people that he did."

She smiled. For once, it seemed to be genuine. "You, a Goth kid? I couldn't imagine it. You're so stylish now. I just couldn't imagine you with black eyeliner and staying up all night with other kids in an abandoned warehouse."

"Well, you don't have much imagination, then, because that's exactly what I was and what I did. I never once saw Derek at one of those things, either, so I would imagine it wasn't his scene."

"No, I would imagine it wasn't." She narrowed her eyes. "Yet, somehow, someway, I think that you and he have a history. I hope you don't mind, but I think I'm going to make it my mission to find out exactly what that history is."

"Knock yourself out." I tried hard to sound calm, cool, and collected, but my voice pitched a little when I talked to her. "You won't find out anything. You'll only discoverthat he and I went to the same school, but didn't run in the same circles. I think that you'll be disappointed when you find out how little we interacted."

"I don't believe you. Why would you punch him unless you had a good reason to?"

"Because…" I didn't quite know how to answer that question. "He said something rude about Slade." I shrugged my shoulders. "He doesn't even know that Slade and I are together, so I guess I shouldn't have taken it quite so personally. But he said that he thought that Slade was guilty as hell and he's dismayed that the charges were going to be dropped against him, and, well, I guess I'm just tired of hearing that. So I punched him. There was really nothing more to it than that."

"Huh. That's kinda ridiculous. After all, most people thought that about Slade. Some people still do, even though it's now obvious that our fearless leader was something of a psychopath. A psychopath with a serious gambling habit at that. But some people still think that Slade had something to do with Jordan's murder. If Derek said something about that, I don't see why you would react so violently."

"I told you, it was the final straw. I'm tired of people just assuming that they know him and assuming that he's guilty. I also think that if Derek is going to be a part of this firm, he probably shouldn't be bad-mouthing former clients like that. I just wanted to put him in his place."

"Okay." She seemed unconvinced. "But I think that you two have some bad blood between you. That's what I think, and I'm usually not wrong about these things."

"Well you're wrong now. Please, I have to get to work."

"Okay, okay." She finally got up to leave. "I have work to do too, of course. But don't think that this conversation is over. It's not. There's something up, and I intend to find out just what it is."

I waved my hand dismissively at her and she finally left.

After she left, though, I shut the door behind her, and I

put my head down on my desk. I tried to calm my beating heart, but I heard Derek standing right outside my door, talking to other co-workers, and I felt myself shaking. I put my head back on my chair and stared at the ceiling. How was I going to get through this? When I didn't want to just punch the guy, but kill him?

I tried to take my mind off of it by poring over the files on my desk. In anticipation of my being sworn in by the State of California, so that I could fully practice law, my firm had piled up a multitude of cases on me. And, of course, there was Margot's case file. It was staring at me accusingly, as if it were beckoning me and taunting me. *You can't win,* the file was saying to me. *You can't win, you're going to blow it, and Slade will never forgive you.*

Slade will never forgive me. There it was – the real reason why I was so stressed out about Margot's case. Sure, if I gave it my all and still lost, there would be no way he could be angry with me. But what if something happened and I made some kind of major mistake, which caused Margot to lose? What if she killed herself, rather than face prison time? What if the cascading wall of dominoes just came tumbling down? I would lose Slade, that's what.

Plus, even if I gave it my all and lost, Slade might be angry with me. It would be irrational anger, of course, but when has anger ever been all that rational?

The fact of the matter was his mother's life was in my hands. I felt trapped. If I pawned the case on somebody else, and that person lost, then Slade would be angry with me for pawning it off. If I took the case on, and I lost, then Slade would be angry with me for losing. I felt like I was in a room with four walls and no doors or windows. Just me in a little tiny box, a box that was getting tinier by the second.

On top of it all, Derek was still outside my door. It

sounded almost like he was intending to knock on the door, but was side-tracked by other people.

Sure enough, in a few minutes, I heard an insistent rapping. I crouched down in my chair, behind my desk, in a defensive position. I was almost thinking that if I made myself as small as possible that Derek would eventually just give up and go away.

But the knocking kept coming. It was then that I realized that I didn't lock the door behind Cindy when she left. I felt vulnerable, like I did in the woods all those years ago. My heart was pounding as loud as the door. I looked down at my hands and realized that I was shaking uncontrollably.

PTSD. I was going to be researching that a lot because of Margot. Dr. Sanderson was an expert in dealing with this disorder. I knew that I had some form of PTSD myself, and it was ever more acute with Derek being around. I knew that PTSD episodes often had a trigger, and, if that trigger was powerful enough, you could be thrown right back into the incident that caused the trauma. Certain smells did that for me for the longest time – the smell of cedar and grass were two smells that caused a powerful physical reaction for years after the incident. The sound of wind whistling through the trees, and of frogs, coyotes, and cicadas – those were the sounds that I heard that night after Derek was through with me. Those were sounds that I could never bear to hear afterwards.

Now here was Derek himself. He was no longer just a piece of my nightmare, but was here in the flesh and blood. And standing outside my door, knocking on it.

I took a deep breath and willed him away.

Unfortunately, he didn't get the hint, because a few minutes later, he was inside my office.

"Serena," he said, flipping on the overhead light. "Why are you here in the dark?"

I looked at him and tried to calm my racing pulse. He looked like any average handsome man that you would see on the street. The kind of guy who women would turn around and look at once he passed by. He might even star in a few fantasies. He wasn't quite as handsome as Slade, but he was very good-looking. It astounded me that somebody who looked like that could be so evil. So vicious. It would be so much easier if the evil men who walked among us would actually look the part, but they didn't. I remembered reading somewhere that Satan would present himself as a beautiful, cherubic child.

Satan might present himself as a beautiful, cherubic child, or he might present himself as a blue-eyed, 6'3" man with fine features and chiseled muscles.

"Derek, I want you to leave me alone," I said to him. "I'm serious. That punch I gave you was your warning, and my way of telling you to back the hell off." I was trying to show him that I wasn't intimidated, but I was acting, of course. In reality, I could hear my heart pounding in my ears, and I had to hide my hands underneath the desk so that he couldn't see how much I was shaking.

To my dismay, he sat down across from me. I tried hard not to cry, and I blinked my eyes rapidly several times in an effort to stem the tide that was threatening. I swallowed hard, and, all of a sudden, the scene in the woods came to me. It was just as if it were happening right at that moment. I could feel him ripping into me savagely, and I could hear myself screaming. I felt the blood rushing down my leg, the blood that was released when he took my virginity. I felt the excruciating pain and humiliation.

He crossed his arms, evidently delighting in seeing me in

such terror. He leaned forward, and I backed away instinctively. "You don't have to be afraid of me," he said in a low voice. "And I would appreciate it if you would call off that fiancé of yours."

"I don't have a fiancé," I said to him.

"Yes you do. That man who you were with told me that you and he were engaged. Anyhow, I don't want him around me anymore."

I narrowed my eyes. Slade had called himself my fiancé, which was strangely exhilarating, even if I knew it was all bullshit. In reality, he wasn't committed to me at all. He was soon going to return to LA, and I was going to be here, and we were going to be nowhere at all. But him saying that we were engaged, even saying that to somebody like Derek, gave me some kind of hope that maybe, just maybe, he was more committed to me than he let on.

I let that thought distract me from the abject terror I was feeling right at that moment, and I felt my heart-rate slow. Slade was with me always, even if he wasn't around physically. He was there to protect me and make sure that people like Derek didn't defeat me. "Slade will be around you as long as you're around me, so get used to it," I told him. "If you think for two seconds that he's just going to let you get away with tormenting me, then you have another thing coming."

"Tormenting you?" He snorted. "I'm not tormenting you. I'm just like you, trying to do my job."

"Your job is owed to Charlotte Boswell and you can't tell me differently. What did she pay you to come out here? Or did she blackmail you somehow?"

"That's none of your goddamned business," he said.

"Oh, but it is. It is. Listen, I don't think that anybody in this firm has any clue about what you really are. And I say 'what,' not 'who,' because I don't consider you to be human. I don't consider you to be an animal, either, because I love all animals and I don't think that any of them are as savage or as evil as you. I consider you to be a form that is lower than anything that is on this earth, and you deserve to be in prison much more than any of our clients." I pointed to the door. "Now, please get the hell out of my office and leave me alone. I know the truth about you and why you're here, and if you don't want the rest of the office also knowing that truth, then I suggest you get out of here and never come back in here again."

I felt better after telling him that little speech, although I could tell that he wasn't moved by it. I knew that my physical reactions to his presence were giving my true feelings away, and, when I saw him don a sly smile, I knew that he wasn't hearing my words. He narrowed his eyes. "Okay, Serena, since you know so much about why I'm here, then you also must know that I have a job to do. A job that I'm being paid very well for doing. So you must also know that I will never leave you alone, because if I did, I would be violating my contract." He stood up. "I'm not going to leave you alone, and I'm going to haunt your every moment in this office. I'm not going to let up, because it's too much damned fun to see you squirm." He shrugged his shoulders. "Plus, I'm being paid well to make sure that your life is a living hell."

I let his words sink in as I gripped the edge of the desk. Of course Charlotte was paying him to harass and torment me. That was the only reason why he was here at the office in the first place, so he couldn't back off. I could already tell that her game was for me to decide between leaving and relegating Margot's fate to the hands of another attorney, or staying at the firm and being tortured by Derek.

I couldn't let Margot go to another attorney, so I just had to stick it out with Derek at the firm. I was damned if I did and damned if I didn't.

I raised my chin and closed my eyes. At the very least, I could get some kind of sense on how he was really feeling. I tuned into his vibrations, and I felt only calm. He wasn't feeling guilty for seeing me so frightened. He wasn't even feeling gleeful about watching me squirm. There was just a nothingness, a void where there should have at least been a conscience.

That was when I knew that he was truly dangerous. He had no feelings. He was simply a hired gun, just another hit man hired by the Garancino family. He had a job to do, and he was going to do it, and there wasn't much that I could do about that. After all, Slade wasn't there at the firm on a daily basis, even though he was now the majority partner. He couldn't just swoop in and protect me every time I felt threatened by Derek. I was well and truly trapped, and that thought made me want to throw up in the trash can next to my desk.

———————

I stayed in my office for the better part of that day. I cowered in there, feeling foolish that I let him defeat me. I was never a girl who was defeated, yet I felt that way. It was just as well, as I had a lot of paperwork to catch up on and phones calls to make. When I finally came out, it was 6 PM and everyone had left for the day.

I felt that I had to get out of there quickly. I packed up my briefcase with the research material that I had found regarding Margot's defense and also with some of the files that I was going to take home and study, and headed out the door of my office.

I was still spooked by the fact that I had tried to get a read on Derek's emotions and felt just nothingness. Was he a true sociopath? I remembered that I was afraid that Slade might be, before I met him. Then, after I met him, I knew that Slade was a good guy. He had true emotions. But this guy...he was truly scary.

Just before I got to the door of the suite, I heard Derek's unmistakable voice behind me. "Serena, this is just perfect. Everyone is gone for the day. Everyone but you and me."

I ignored him, and kept on walking. I could see the suite door right in front of me, and I knew that it was just a matter of time before I was out by the elevators where there would be plenty of people milling about. This was a large office building and I was a bit surprised that everyone had left my own office this early – there was always somebody who worked a bit late.

"Serena, I just addressed you. Turn around and look at me."

I just kept walking, but I felt his hands on my shoulders. The icy fear that had gripped me earlier was soon spreading all over the rest of my body. *Just keep on walking, just keep on walking.*

He put his arm around my neck, and, for just a moment, I froze completely. "You like being hurt, I know you do. You love the pain, the humiliation, the fear. Don't think that I don't know all about your lifestyle in New York City. I would love to be your master."

It was then that I did the only thing that I could think of doing in that situation. I shoved my heel right in his crotch and he crumpled to the ground. I then ran to the door of the suite, and proceeded to run down the stairs. All 50 flights. I took off my shoes and just ran.

As I got into my car, I tried not to think of the encounter with Derek in the office suite. All that I had to concentrate on was getting the keys in the ignition of the car, putting the car into gear, and driving off.

I somehow managed to put my shaking hands on the steering wheel, while turning the key of the ignition. How I managed that, I don't really know. All that I knew was that I soon found myself barreling down the road while wiping away my tears. My mind was a jumble of so many things…I knew that I couldn't tell Slade that Derek had intimidated me, because I didn't know how he would react. I also knew that I couldn't possibly quit my job, because it was so important to me to represent Margot. I had to do that for Slade and for Margot herself.

Dammit! How did that bastard find out about my "lifestyle" in New York City? Why was that any of his business? And the thought that he "wanted to be my master" was a thought that I couldn't even begin to comprehend. There was nothing sicker, in my mind, than what he had just proposed.

As I slowed my racing heart and got my shaking hands under control, I knew that what had happened that day was something that might continue to happen in the future.

Even with this revelation coming to light, though, I was also aware, that I could never run.

Chapter Thirteen

When I got home, I found Slade in his office. He apparently was on a Skype call with somebody overseas, because he was talking to somebody on a screen and was speaking a different language. I was briefly fascinated by his fluency in this particular language, which sounded like German. I looked at my watch and saw that it read 7 PM, which would mean that this person Slade was speaking with was up at a very late hour. By my rough calculations, it was in the early morning there.

I wondered if there was some trouble brewing on that front. That's all you need right now – Slade having problems at his company.

Slade's voice was getting louder, and then, just like that, he wasn't talking anymore. I went into the office after I heard him stop speaking, and he was just staring at the computer screen, which was blank. He jumped a little when he heard me come in.

"Serena," he said, coming over to me and putting his arms around me. "It's good to see you. I'm glad your home." The dogs came up to me, and excitedly started to try to jump on me. I pet them absent-mindedly while Slade had his arms wrapped around me.

"I didn't interrupt anything, did I?" That was my polite way of inquiring about the Skype call. Whatever was happening, it didn't seem to be good news.

"Not really. I was just speaking with an overseas investor, and apparently one of our patents is about to be denied over there in Germany. That poor guy has been up all night trying to figure out how to circumvent their government on this."

"I'm sorry to hear that."

"It's not that big of a deal. It wasn't one of our marquee drugs, so I'm not going to get too upset about it." He kissed me, a long, deep kiss, and then he backed off of me slightly. "I'm more interested in what's going on with you. You don't seem to be quite yourself right now."

I had made up my mind that I wasn't going to tell Slade about my encounters with Derek. If Slade knew that Derek was giving me as much trouble as he was, then there was the possibility that he would try to make me quit my job. I just couldn't do that to Margot. So, I was going to keep quiet about what was really going on.

I shrugged my shoulders. "It's been a long day. You know, I was away from the office for a few days, and I had a pile of work to catch up on. I'm sure you're quite familiar with the concept."

He smiled. "Me? Nah. My life has always been charmed and hard work has never factored into the equation at all." Then he winked and I had to smile.

I spent the rest of that evening just making some small talk with Slade over dinner about different things. I didn't necessarily want to talk about anything stressful, and I got the feeling that he was the same.

Eventually, however, I did feel more comfortable about talking about what was on my mind. Not about Derek, necessarily, but about my revelation about perhaps needing a therapist for my own PTSD. "Dr. Sanderson is going to evaluate Margot, and perhaps she could also use him as a therapist," I told Slade. "And maybe I should think about doing the same."

He nodded. "I was wondering about that. It seems that, ever since Derek came back into the picture, you've seemed just a little bit off. I don't want you to go through your life afraid. I'm going to do what I can to keep that bastard in line, and I really wish that you could just quit to get away from him." He looked down at his glass of wine, and then took a sip. "If I knew what Charlotte would do if you did quit, then I would almost certainly be all for you just getting out of there."

Oh, of course. The Charlotte factor. Outside of the fact that I didn't want to desert Margot, Charlotte was still the reason why I was trapped working with Derek. There was always the danger that she could come after me if things didn't go quite her way. "It doesn't matter, Slade. I want to keep working there. I really do think that I can do Margot's case justice, much more than other attorney. Remember, I have an uncanny knack in picking the right jury, and that's going to be absolutely crucial in this case."

"I understand that, but I also think that Derek is causing you too much stress." He shook his head. "I'd like to kill that bastard. I really would." His eyes were flashing, and I knew that he was at least partially serious. Not that Slade would *actually* kill Derek, but that he was tempted to.

"Hey," I said, putting my hand on his. "It's going to be okay. I'm a big girl, I can hold my own, and I need to face this down. I need to face it down and know that I'm strong enough to get through this. I love that you're in my corner and that I can count on you, but, believe me, it's all going to be for the best. What happened to me all those years ago is something that has haunted me, and now I have the chance to really face it. Derek working with me is the best thing that ever happened."

In a way, I was lying to Slade when I said those words. Working with Derek was something that definitely didn't seem to be a blessing. Yet, at the same time, I knew that I was also partially right – I had to face him and I had to get stronger about it. If I could do that, then I could finally start to live my life completely without fear.

"You're a remarkable woman," he said, as he came over to my side of the dinner table. "You know that?"

I smiled. "So I've heard. So you've told me."

"I have?" he asked me softly. "Well, let me tell you again."

He took my legs and spread them on the chair. He kissed me as he wrapped my legs around his back tightly. I was wearing a skirt, like I usually do at work, but I also was wearing thigh-highs which were held up by a garter and high-heeled shoes. He massaged my inner thighs as he looked down at my garter lustfully.

"Do you like?" I asked him.

"Oh, yeah," he said as he kissed my inner thigh. He continued to massage my thigh as his other hand made its way to my thong panties. He kneeled down in front of me as he casually brought down both of my knee-highs and my panties. My legs were still stretched out in front of me, and he held me by my feet. He kissed my calves and my thighs and his tongue made its way to my clit. He hoisted me up on the table, which excited me, because his cock was now on the same level as my nether-region.

He lightly pushed me down on the table as he unbuttoned my shirt and unhooked my bra. His hands stroked my breasts and nipples, and he sucked and nibbled on them while his hands swirled around my clit and inner folds. He kissed my neck and teased my nether-parts with his enormous and proud manhood, which sprung forth from his pants. I unbuttoned his shirt and ran my fingers along his hard pecs and eight-pack abs. He kissed me on the lips, and I ran my fingers through his thick hair.

With a sigh, I felt him enter me slowly, and then pick up his rhythm. I lay backwards on the table again, and brought him to me. My legs were wrapped around him tightly, and they clenched his backside as he continued to stroke in and out of me. He rooted deeply inside of me, hitting my G-Spot and making me scream in ecstasy. I had one sweet release, and then another and another, in rapid succession. I briefly thought that I would lose consciousness, because my orgasms were that powerful.

He finally had his own release, and he kissed my lips and my eyelids and face. "Well," he said, "I'm guessing we're going to have to wash this table pretty good before we eat on it again," he joked.

"Indeed."

Chapter Fourteen

The next few weeks went by like a flash. I was finding, more and more, that all the glaring media attention that Slade's case was garnering was getting to be a pain to deal with. It seemed like, every time I turned around, there was a reporter that was calling me, ostensibly to get the dirt on Margot's case. I never told them anything, of course, but they kept calling anyhow. And once again, just like when Slade was accused of murder, the pundits were talking about this case pretty much non-stop. This was a case that excited the pundit class even more than the murder case, because Slade was clearly guilty of covering up the murder of Hugh and disposing of his body, and the media was absolutely salivating that he would finally get his comeuppance that he, in their eyes, so richly deserved.

For Slade's part, he shrugged all the attention off. He also didn't appear to be taking the charges against him very seriously. "Jackson has it all under control," he said. "And my PR team is starting to bend the media attention the other way. They aren't there yet, but the media's narrative is beginning to question the prosecutor in this case, and the new narrative is starting to become that this is all a witch-hunt. That the prosecutor desperately wanted to pin Jordan's murder on me, and, since the prosecutor's office couldn't do that, they're going all out against me on this case. We'll see if that new narrative sticks."

Indeed, Slade seemed impressed that his PR team was able to spin the entire case in that manner. They were completely on the offensive, on Slade's behalf, sending surrogate after surrogate to the talk shows to try to get the story out that the prosecutor simply has it in for Slade. And the media was starting to buy it. Slowly but surely, the talking heads were being less hard on Slade and there were even a few hosts who entertained the notion that Slade was simply being railroaded again, by an overzealous prosecutor, mainly because he was a mini-celebrity and had just been exonerated of a heinous crime. The prosecutors, so the narrative was going, were trying to take revenge on Slade because they were so upset about letting him slip through their fingers in the murder of Jordan.

So, that was a development that gave all of us a bit of breathing room. Not that the media wasn't still obsessed, but they were slightly less so, and were getting even less so every day. I was able to concentrate more on Margot's case and less on what was going on with Slade and his case.

Derek was still an issue, and, even though I had intended to return to my house, I found myself making excuses not to. Every day, though, Slade asked me about him and how he was treating me, and I honestly told him that Derek was not that big of a problem anymore. He was still around, of course, but he hadn't cornered me like he did that one evening when we were all alone in the office suite.

I was also making headway on Margot's case. I had set her up with an appointment with Dr. Sanderson, and he evaluated her and decided that she did have PTSD. He also determined that she had a reasonable belief that Hugh was going to rape her, because of what had happened previously to her in prison. He agreed to keep seeing Margot on a regular basis, so it was just a matter of scheduling depositions with this doctor and having the prosecutor ask him questions under oath. They also scheduled to have her evaluated by their own expert. Basically, it was going to come down to dueling experts, and the jury was going to have to decide which expert was more credible.

My relationship with Slade was also continuing, and was deepening by the day. We were in a good place, which felt right. After all that we had gone through, it was really about time that we had a little bit of happiness. Happiness was something that was fleeting, I had always found, and I wanted to just hold onto it tightly. Just put both of my hands around our happiness and squeeze it.

Then, one day, I went to get my mail – I had opened up a PO Box when I went to stay with Slade originally, and I went to it every other day. It was then that I discovered that Slade and I weren't the only ones who were trying hard to grab onto happiness. Luke and Dalilah were finally making things official, and they were to be married at her father's estate in Montauk.

I went to talk with Slade that day, after finding out that I had been invited to this wedding. "Slade," I said to him. "I have to travel to New York in a month. My brother Luke is finally getting married."

He raised a single eyebrow. "*You're* going to see your brother?" he asked accusingly.

I suddenly felt shy. "Well, I was going to ask you to go with me, but…" I felt weird asking him, for some reason.

"Well, what?"

"Nothing. Would you like to go?"

He smiled big. "I thought you would never ask. We'll take my plane and we'll make a weekend of it."

I nodded my head, feeling foolish that I was too shy to ask him to accompany me to New York. We had been together for months by this time, and I still was never quite sure where I stood with him. "That will be fun," I said. "It will definitely be a much-needed vacation for us."

"It's a date." He came over to me and put a spoon in my mouth. It was a delicious sauce that he was making for some pasta. He had definitely developed some skills in cooking vegan foods, and I loved that about him. He was really trying to accommodate me. That was one of the things that we did together - cooking. It was a relaxing thing and it gave us a chance to really bond with each other.

I took a deep breath as I inhaled his scent. It was always intoxicating to me, and I always felt, when I was with him, that I had just met him. I hoped that being with him would never get old.

"Are you going to have Jackson make a motion to the court to allow you to leave the state?"

He shrugged. "I guess so. I don't think that it's a big deal, because the judge didn't put a condition on my bond that I'm to stay in the jurisdiction."

"That's certainly promising." His judge, Judge Richards, seemed to be a fair sort. So far, there hadn't been any major rulings that went against him, and we were both hopeful that he could beat his charge.

"It is." He put his arms around me, and I felt the warmth of his skin on mine. "Mmmmm, I'm really hungry, but I'd love to just take you upstairs and do things to you that you've never had done. Which, admittedly, doesn't leave much." He grinned as I slapped him lightly with the kitchen towel that I had in my hand.

"Let's eat first," I said, "and then we can do things to each other."

We set the table and both of us sat down to eat. The dogs were at my feet, and Bella was whining softly. They were almost fully grown, and they had really developed their own personalities. Bella was more demanding of my time, attention and love. Gigi was more laid-back about everything, being seemingly content to just watch the world go by. Whenever there was begging at the dinner table, it was usually Bella leading the way on that.

I fed both dogs from the table, and they seemed to inhale the food. I smiled at both of them and talked to them. They seemed to understand every word I said, or, at least, they pretended to. Their ears were perked up, which meant that the ears on both dogs were pointed to the ceiling.

We drank our wine and he asked me how things were going with Margot's case.

"They're doing fine," I said. "Of course, the real test will come when the trial actually happens. As you know, it's set for trial in two months." I shook my head. "I don't know what to expect at trial at all. If we get the right jury, then we have a chance."

"You're very good at that, right?"

"Yes. Because I'm an empath, I can usually feel the emotions of the people on that jury panel. I know who's being sincere and who isn't. Generally, I do." I was still a bit upset that I had let Malcolm slip in under my radar. I had no idea that he was diabolical, and that stung me. Thus far, though, Malcolm was the only person who had completely fooled me. I usually was able to peg just about everyone else around me.

I had also found that I had an easier time "reading" strangers than people who I knew well. I guessed that was because I had no pre-conceived notions about strangers, and I hadn't yet allowed them to influence me. That was always the problem with trying to get a perfect read on people I knew, because most of the time, they wore a mask that they showed to the outside world. It was this mask that complicated things for me. Sometimes, I had a hard time reconciling what was roiling beneath a person's exterior with what was being shown to the world.

"Well, then, good. Your expert seems to know what he's doing, and I know that she's going to be in excellent hands with you."

"Hmmmmm, speaking of excellent hands," I said as I gripped Slade's hands in my own. "You have the most amazing hands I've ever encountered."

He smiled. "I could say the same about you."

He picked me and carried me to the bed. I put my hand on his crotch, and his manhood was standing at full attention. I massaged it lightly through his pants, and then I unbuckled his belt and unzipped his fly. I pushed him down on the bed, and got down on my knees. I freed his enormous cock and put it into my mouth greedily. I sucked and licked the length of his shaft, and he groaned. My lips and tongue where working the head of his manhood, while my fingers massaged his jewels. My tongue made its way down to them, and I lightly bit and sucked each one. His groaning became louder and louder in my ears. I could feel that he was about to climax in my mouth, so I swallowed some pre-cum and abruptly let up. I didn't want this to end so soon.

I stood up, and stroked his chest some more. He put his arms around me, and brought my face to his and kissed me tenderly. His lips soon became more insistent and raw and passionate, though. I felt as if his mouth was devouring my own. I pulled off my shirt and pants, and our two naked bodies were melded together on the bed. He pushed me over so that I was on my back, and then he hovered over me for a few minutes. I sighed as he kissed my breasts and neck and then plunged his cock hard into me. I felt the familiar sensation of being filled, and, as he slowly and surely made his way in and out, I felt myself peaking. I groaned and cried out, my head shaking from side to side. I felt him come inside of me, and I felt complete.

Chapter Fifteen

We left for Luke's wedding on a Thursday, after I dropped my two precious babies off at their doggie hotel. I knew that they loved being there, because they got to play with all the other dogs during the day.

Margot's trial was looming, and I was getting nervous about it. I didn't want to show Slade that, though. I was determined that he and I were going to have a good time in New York. I was genuinely happy for Luke, of course, and thought that he deserved all the happiness in the world.

Slade and I boarded his private plane, and shared a bottle of champagne while we waited to take off. As I sat there next to him, though, I could tell that there was something on his mind. He didn't quite seem to be his usual exuberant self – in fact, he seemed rather quiet and reserved.

"What's going on?" I asked him.

"What do you mean?"

"I can sense that something is just a bit off with you. I

don't know what it is, though." I couldn't quite put a finger on his emotions, but I felt that he was just a bit scattered. His emotions were right there on the surface, and I wondered why I was feeling that he was extremely anxious.

"There's no hiding things from you." He made that statement and it seemed that he was unhappy. "I wish that I could hide things from you sometimes."

I cleared my throat. "What are you trying to hide from me?"

"I didn't want to say anything. After all, we're going to New York to celebrate the wedding of your brother. The last thing that I wanted to do was to put a wet blanket over the proceedings."

I felt alarmed and I had no idea why. "A wet blanket? I don't understand. Is there something going on with your case that you aren't telling me?"

He shook his head. "No. Nothing like that." He bit his lip and looked out the window of the plane. Then he turned to face me again. "Charlotte is…"

"Charlotte is – what? What is she? She's a psycho-woman. That much is for sure. But what are you trying to say?"

"Give me a chance, and I'll tell you."

I waited for him to speak. I didn't try to fill the air with the sound of my own voice, because there had to be some pressure on him to tell me what was on his mind.

"Charlotte is…concerning me these days. She knows that I'm going to release things about her that would destroy her career, if she makes a move against you. She's been calling the shots, as much as she can, because I have every-thing to lose if she decides to call off our agreement. I apol-ogize for that, too."

"You're protecting me, and that's what's important."

"Yes." He shook his head. "I'm protecting you. And I'll always protect you. You can count on that, and you can count on me."

I took his hand and looked him in the eye. "Slade, I know that. I know that you're always interested in my welfare, and I love that about you."

He looked at his glass of champagne, and then took a sip. He looked up at the ceiling, and shook his head again. "It's just that I can never quite get a decent read on Charlotte. She's a hard one to figure out, just because she's certifiably nuts. That's the worst kind to deal with, because you aren't dealing with rationality."

"So, what are you saying?" From the look on Slade's face, I knew that there was something amiss with Charlotte. I didn't quite know what that "something amiss" was, though.

"Well, I don't actually know quite yet. I've been in touch with her, which is a necessity, because I need to keep trying to get a read on where she's at. She's been blowing smoke because you haven't lived in your home for all of these months, which negates the reason why she had Derek move in next door to you. She is also upset about the fact that Derek has not really been harassing you at the workplace. She apparently is getting progress reports from Derek about what's going on."

"What does all this mean?"

"It means that I don't quite know where she stands. I've been standing up for you, of course, every time she gets on her high horse about how her plan isn't working the way that she wants it to. Even so, I get the feeling that she's losing patience with the whole arrangement. And that makes her extremely dangerous, as far as you're concerned."

I lay back on the leather seat of the plane and took a sip of my champagne. It was a dry champagne, evidently extremely high-dollar. It had a long French name that I hadn't heard of, but I could recognize expensive champagne when I tasted it. And I was definitely tasting expensive champagne. "She won't make a move. She has too much to lose. I saw the write-up she got in *Variety* this week, and there's a lot of Oscar buzz around her new role. I can't imagine that she would give all that up just to get her revenge on me for stealing you away."

"If I was dealing with a rational person, I would say that you are absolutely correct. She has a lot on the line, as far as her reputation in Hollywood." He made a bridge with his hands and stared at them. There was something else that was on his mind, and I had to find out just what that was.

I put my arm around him and threw one leg over his lap. "You aren't dealing with a rational person, though, are you?"

He sighed and lay back on the seats. He spread his legs in front of him and put his hands behind his head. "No. Well, it's not even that." He shook his head. "She's seeing, with me, the power of good PR. The power of a good spokesperson, which is what I have with Jackson. She's seeing that the media is starting to come around in their coverage of me and what I did. And she's starting to think that she's impervious herself. That, even if the reports about her craziness and her connection to the murder were to get out to the press, she might be able to spin it in a way that actually helps her."

I started to feel the icy tendrils of fear creep into my veins as I looked at Slade. His face was definitely worried, and when I closed my eyes to tune into his vibrations, I felt it from him. I felt more anxiety coming from him than I ever had. He wasn't this anxious when he was accused of Jordan's murder. He wasn't this anxious even when he was determined to serve his time for that murder. This was an anxiety that was almost palpable. It was something that I felt that I could reach out and grab if I really wanted to.

"I don't even want to ask this, but I will. What happens if she decides to take the chance? What if she decides just to tell you to release that report, and she'll deal with the fallout?"

When he looked at me with those beautiful green eyes, I knew that I was possibly in trouble. "What do you think will happen if she decides to take that chance? Right now, the only thing that is stopping her from putting out a hit on you is the fact that I have that report, and she doesn't want to slow her momentum in Hollywood. If she decides, in her sick little head, that my releasing this report won't kill her career, then she's dangerous. She'll have nothing to lose."

Nothing to lose. Those were the three worst words that I had ever heard. It's scary to hear that somebody has nothing to lose, when that somebody has the power to make you become dead. "Okay, well, let's go over this scenario. Charlotte decides that she's okay with you releasing damning information about her to the press. What happens next?"

He shook his head. "Dammit, I need to protect you, no matter what I have to do. I wish that there was some way that I could just take your place, and that Charlotte could put the hit on me, not you. In fact, I've asked that of her – to take me, and leave you alone. She won't do that, though. In her twisted mind, she and I still have the possibility of a bright future together. She won't ever give up that dream. She won't give up that dream."

"I don't understand. She tried to put you in prison for

the rest of your life. That would have put a kibosh on that dream, wouldn't it have?"

"Of course." He paused. "Your mistake is assuming that Charlotte is thinking like a rational person, which she's not. She's sick in the head, therefore, her thinking doesn't have to make sense. It doesn't make sense to me, either, to be honest with you. I suppose it's not supposed to."

"Well, if there's a hit on me, then we can run, right?"

"I wish. No, her family had tendrils everywhere. I couldn't ever chance that, anyhow. I would like to think that I could protect you, 100%, but I need to be realistic. It's very difficult to run from a mob hit. Look at all the people who are in witness protection – they still have to spend their entire lives running and hiding, and looking over their shoulders. They still end up dead a lot of the times, even when they're protected by the FBI. No, running isn't a good option."

"Then what is?"

He swallowed hard. "I'm trying to formulate a good plan, but I keep hitting road blocks wherever I turn."

"Well, then, I can do one thing. I've been meaning to do it, anyhow. But I'll move back to my home. I can live next to Derek. I'm starting to feel stronger when I'm around him at work. I've stood up for myself against him. If Charlotte is making noise about backing out of your deal with her, partially because she wants me to be stuck living next to that sociopath, then okay. I'll go back there."

Slade appeared not to hear me. He was staring off into space, the glass of champagne still in his hand. Then he finally looked over at me and I could see the worry. "I hate to say it, but that would help. It would buy time, anyhow. It'll buy time until I can figure out what to do, and how far to go."

"How far to go?"

"Yes. How far to go. So far, I only have the threat to her career in my back pocket. That's still a powerful threat – she's seen other rising stars who were derailed because they had a bad reputation with their peers and directors. That's keeping her in line so far. I just don't know how long it's going to continue to work, and that's what scares the living crap out of me."

"Back up. What did you mean by how far to go?"

He shook his head. "Nothing. I didn't mean anything by that."

I closed my eyes and I felt some degree of deception coming from him. It was a vague, unsettling feeling, but I got the unmistakable impression that there was something he wasn't telling me. Something huge that he wasn't telling me.

"Slade, if you're thinking of doing something drastic, then I have to advise against that. Let's just say that you decide to somehow do Charlotte in for good. Don't think for a second that you can get away with that. Her mob family will literally kill you, and then they'll come after me, because I was the original target. All that will accomplish will be to make both of us dead."

"Believe me, I've been tempted to do just that. Turn the hit around on her. But you're right about one thing – doing that would start a war. There's not much chance that I could do that without her family finding out that it was me, and then I'll be in danger and you will too. So, no. That won't work."

"That won't work, but what will?"

He shook his head. "We're just going to have to keep doing what we're doing for now, and I do think that it will help her frame of mind if you were living back in your old house. As much as I hate to ask you to do that, it's the only thing that I can think of working right now."

"Does she really think that she can be revealed as a murderess, and that she can be revealed as having border-line personality disorder, and there won't be any damage to her career? I don't get that at all. Young actors are revealed to having had a wild past all the time, but none actually killed somebody when they were young."

"No, that's true. But Mark Wahlberg was charged with attempted murder for an unprovoked attack on a Viet-namese man. You hardly ever heard about that, and that incident hasn't exactly affected his career."

"Charged with attempted murder is much different than being guilty of actual murder. I still can't believe that she got off with such a light sentence. I know that she was a juvenile at the time, but still. She's lucky that she only had to serve time in juvenile hall, and that her record was expunged when she became of age."

Slade rolled his eyes. "Do you think that her family's influence had something to do with that? And you're right – anybody else who would be convicted of such a crime wouldn't get the preferential treatment that Charlotte has undoubtedly received. That's what makes her dangerous, too – she's always been able to get away with her bullshit, because her family is so powerful. I get the feeling that she thinks that she'll beat this too. That if I went to the media with her record, she'll just be able to spin her way out of it with the media and her adoring fans. I think that she's delu-sional, especially because her current reputation is that of 'America's Sweetheart.'"

"Well, I don't really know what to do or what to tell you. What I do know is that there's very little that we can do about all of this right now. All that I want to think about, for the next few days, is you and me in New York City, and how happy I am for my brother. I'm anxious for you to meet the whole family, too. Including my father's new wife. We all had an issue, at first, with him finding somebody to spend the rest of his life with, just because none of us has really gotten over losing mom in the way that we did. But she's pretty cool, and so is the rest of my family."

"Does your father's new wife have any kids?"

"She has two daughters, both a few years younger than me. Bailey is one of the daughters, and she's a pretty girl with purple hair and black fingernails. The other one's name is Rayanne. I think that they're identical twins, although they don't really look like it. Rayanne is a bit more conventional than Bailey."

Truth be told, I had an affinity for Bailey. She reminded me of myself at that age – purple hair, nose ring, tattoos and a fuck-you attitude. I got the feeling that she didn't take much shit from anyone in her life, and that made me admire her all the more. I didn't know much else about her, though.

From what I understood about Bailey and her sister, they were somewhat like my twin brothers Christopher and Mark. Chris was a rock star, or at least he played a rock star in his mind, and he was extremely troubled. I knew why – he was only alive because our mother sacrificed her life for him. He also saw her dead, as well as seeing all the other people in that McDonald's massacre dead. That affected him immensely, I knew, although I didn't quite know the depths of darkness that was in his soul.

I took Slade's hand and looked him in the eye. "Whatever happens with Charlotte, we'll deal with it. We can run." I knew that he had a house in Lake Como, Italy, and I had to think that there were worse things in life than having to live in a gorgeous resort town like that one. Living in a place that was surrounded by water and the Italian Alps, while also being close to quaint little towns, was something that sounded like heaven to me right at that moment.

He shook his head. "We can run, sure, but I really don't want us to be looking over our shoulder for the rest of our lives." He paused while he stared at his hands pensively. "And Serena, I can't lose you. I don't think that you know what a difference you've made in my life. Since I met you, I've had a reason to get up in the morning. I mean, I've always had a reason to get up in the morning before, but that reason was not fulfilling for me. I was all about the business and getting ahead. Discovering new drugs to bring to market, making enormous profits quarter in and quarter out – those were the things that gave me a high before. Now, it's different. I feel that I've finally found the one thing that matters."

As he swallowed hard while carefully avoiding my eyes, I knew that Slade was not only sincere but was expressing something that was hard for him. He continued to look worried, and that worried me even more. Something had changed for him, and it had changed just recently. Something was going on with Charlotte. Perhaps it was just a feeling that he had, or maybe she said something concrete to make him believe that she was going to throw caution to wind and come after me. But it was definitely something.

"Slade, what is it? Is there a credible threat that I need to know about?"

He looked at me for what seemed to be the longest time, just staring at me with those beautiful green eyes of his. I closed my eyes and clearly felt deception coming from him. He was going to lie to me, and I knew why – this weekend wasn't about stress, or it shouldn't be. It was a time just to forget all about Margot and Charlotte and Derek.

Finally, instead of just coming out and telling me what was on his mind, he just shook his head. "Not right now. I'm so sorry, Serena, but I just feel that now is not the time."

I hated that. I had always hated that. Somebody clearly has something to say, yet they don't say it. You're left with knowing that something is out there, something bad, but not knowing exactly what that bad thing is.

"Slade, I know what you're thinking. You're thinking that if you talk to me about whatever is on your mind, that the weekend in New York will be ruined. But if you don't tell me what's going on, I'm going to wonder. It's going to be built up in my head the entire time. I'm going to be looking over my shoulder the whole time that we're in Montauk. This should be a time when there's nothing but happiness and love and light surrounding everyone. It certainly shouldn't be a time when I'm looking around, half expecting there to be men with guns shooting up the place."

Slade smiled and, just for a second, I thought that what-ever was on his mind wasn't as bad as I was thinking. "I believe that somebody has seen too many movies. A mob hit doesn't necessarily work like that, my love. They're not going to be recklessly coming into a wedding and mowing everyone down. Well, unless your name is Pretty Boy Floyd and you lived during prohibition." He was referring to the "Union Station Massacre" in Kansas City, Missouri, in which law enforcement officials were gunned down by mobsters, right in the public view. "And even they didn't do anything to a wedding party."

"No, but some terrorists did. Right?"

"I believe so. But the Italians aren't quite as ruthless as terrorists or even as ruthless as different ethnic mafias. They have some respect, and they're usually only interested in targeted hits."

I shook my head. I was an innocent person. So was Slade, for that matter. How I possibly became the target of a hit was something that I couldn't even fathom. It was all because Charlotte was a mafia princess. I guessed that she really had control over who her family hit.

"Slade, you're avoiding my concerns and questions. What do I have to worry about?"

He finally sighed and shook his head. "Nothing. I mean, I don't know. It's just that her agent called me the other day."

"Her agent? I don't quite understand."

"Yes, her agent. Her agent knows all about Charlotte's past. She knows about the murder and about Charlotte's mental problems. She's been trying to keep it all under wraps, and she's done one helluva job with that all these years. Her agent is somebody who has a lot of power in Hollywood. And she called me."

I swallowed hard. I looked down at my hands, and noticed how much they were shaking. I felt like I was in the presence of Derek, all alone. I had the sinking feeling that somebody gets when they're facing certain peril. Like when inmates take that long, long walk to the death chamber. That's what I was feeling like.

"What did she say to you?" I asked in a tiny voice. I almost didn't want to ask the question, but I knew that I had to.

"She expressed concern. She told me that she knew what evidence I had that confirms Charlotte is crazy, and she told me that Charlotte had been asking her, the agent, to go public with it. Charlotte and her agent are working, even as we speak, on how to spin this story once it gets into the public."

"Why did she call you?"

"She wanted me to try to talk Charlotte out of doing it. She told me that she thought that I had some influence over Charlotte, and she thought that I might be able to talk some sense into her."

"I see." I felt all the blood rush from my head and it felt like it left my body completely. I suddenly felt cold, clammy and hollow. "So, Charlotte is…"

"She's ready to back out of our agreement. I don't necessarily know why. I need to get to the bottom of it, and I will, once you and I get back to LA. My fear is that…"

"I haven't suffered enough." I nodded my head. "That's what she wants. She wants me to suffer. She wants to know that I'm spooked and afraid. She hates that you're protecting me from Derek. She hates that you're protecting me at all. I know her game, believe it or not."

Slade finally nodded his head slowly. "Yes. I think that you might be right about that. And I'm torn. I'm torn, because I don't want you to suffer at all. I want to make sure that nothing bad ever happens to you. But, ironically, the thing to do is to make Charlotte believe that you're suffering. That might make her back off. Then again, I don't know that it will. Charlotte tends to make a decision and stick to it, no matter what. If she has her mind made up that she's going to back out of our deal, then I don't know that I can stop it. At that point, we might have to go on the run, although I don't think that we can run far enough or fast enough to get away from her."

"Okay." I felt helpless, like there wasn't a damn thing that could be done about Charlotte. If she was determined to make me "pay" for the sin of loving Slade, then she was going to do it. There wasn't much that could really stop her, if the threat of the whole world knowing that she murdered somebody when she was very young couldn't derail her. What Slade had on her was powerful stuff. I didn't think that Charlotte's career could really survive it. I had always heard that there is no bad publicity, but an exception can be made when somebody had actually murdered a person in cold blood.

Both of us sat back in our seats and sipped our champagne. Neither of us talked for the next few hours. I was too lost in thought and I knew that Slade was as well.

Right before the plane landed, though, I knew I had to talk to Slade one more time about Charlotte. "Slade, you're not thinking…" I shook my head.

"Yes, I have thought about that. I already know what you're going to say. And, yes, I have thought about giving Charlotte what she wants. I would be absolutely miserable, but if it ensures your safety, I would do it." Once again, his eyes didn't meet mine.

My heart started to pound when he said those words. I felt hot tears rush to my eyes, even as the city came into view. I wanted to tell him not to do that, under any circumstances. That I would take my chances out in the world, and if Charlotte hit me, she hit me. But I knew that Slade wasn't thinking like that. He was thinking about all that I was going through, seeing Derek every day. He was thinking about my safety and my life.

He was gripping his glass, which was empty, and he picked up a tumbler and filled it with some gin. "Let's not think about any of this over the weekend, okay? Charlotte might be ready to do something drastic, but I don't think it's going to happen within the next 72 hours. And meeting your family is an important thing for me. I want to be accepted by them, because I still believe that you and I are going to be together. Please, don't worry about Charlotte or anything else."

I nodded my head, but said nothing. I had no words.

The plane was descending rapidly, and Slade looked over at me. "When this plane touches down, it ends the discussion of Charlotte, at least until we leave New York. So, if there's anything that you need to ask me about her, ask it now."

I didn't say anything, but I couldn't control the tears that started to stream down my cheeks. "You and I..." I shook my head, unable to say more.

"We have a future together." When he said those words, though, he said them weakly. As if he didn't really believe those words himself. "I believe that, and I want you to believe that, too. I need you to believe that I'm going to find a way out of this for both of us. I need you to believe that, Serena."

"I believe that," I said, although my voice sounded just as weak as his. "I believe that."

"Good." Then he smiled. "Now, I already arranged for a limo to pick us up and take us out to our hotel. The driver will be waiting for us with a big sign, so keep a lookout."

I smiled, although it was forced. "I'll keep a lookout."

The plane landed and we walked out onto the tarmac. It was autumn, so it was getting cold. The time had just switched over, so it was also getting dark, even though it was only 4 PM. I smelled the air, feeling comforted. This was home to me. I loved San Diego for the weather and for the fact that it was relatively uncongested. "Relatively" was the operative word there, of course, as San Diego was a large city and had a lot of traffic problems of its own. But it was still nothing like New York. Yet, New York was the one place where I truly felt at home. I had lived there, or in the general area, for almost a decade.

Slade smiled. "I guess it's good that we brought our heavier coats. We certainly don't need them in California, although I think that they're going to come in handy for us on this trip."

"Good thing the wedding is during the day. It's on the beach, and it's supposed to get to 80 degrees on Saturday. Right now, though, it certainly does seem cool."

"I know how we can keep warm," Slade said with a sly smile. "And wait until you see the suite that I booked at The Four Seasons. It will take your breath away. It takes *my* breath away, so I can just imagine yours."

I smiled as we sipped more champagne in the limo. As the limo meandered through the crowded streets, and I was able to really take in the scene around me, I started to feel calmer. Charlotte was across the country, as was Derek, and Margot's case was still about a month away, barring any unforeseen circumstances. This city felt like a world away from all of my problems.

When we got to The Four Seasons and we checked into our suite, I found that Slade wasn't exaggerating. This suite *did* take my breath away. 100%. The ceilings were easily 20 feet tall, and there was a wall of floor to ceiling windows that had a magnificent view of the New York City skyline. As I walked from room to room, I saw that the view was panoramic, because every single room had a different view of the city. As it was already dark, the lights on all the buildings were twinkling. There was a grand piano in an alcove, and there were two jacuzzi tubs, one of which was so large that it was like a small pool. Everywhere I looked, there were bouquets of flowers, candles, and opulent works of art.

"What do you think?" Slade asked as he came up

behind me and wrapped his arms around me. "Does this suite meet your expectations?"

I smiled. "Does it. I've never quite seen anything like this. At least I haven't in a hotel." Of course, Slade's mansions in San Diego and Los Angeles were much more well-appointed than this suite, but, for a hotel suite, Slade was right. This place was truly magnificent.

Slade made both of us a drink and we settled in next to the fireplace. He turned on the gas fireplace and put his arm around me on the couch. "I'm glad that you like this place. It's really difficult to book, but we're lucky that there isn't a whole lot going on in this city this weekend. I mean, there is, there always is, but there isn't a heavier-than-usual crowd to deal with like there would be during the holidays."

"Have you been to this city often?"

"As often as I can. I've been here quite a bit for business, of course, but I've also managed to visit this city when my mom lived here, after Hugh was killed." He shook his head. "I regret sending her away now. It makes her look guilty as hell."

"Yes, but we can also explain all of that away."

"I hope that you're right. In the meantime, let's not think about any of that. I'm starving, so let's go to the restaurant and have some dinner. And then, after dinner, we'll have dessert." At that, he growled in my ear. "And just wait until you see the dessert I have planned for you."

"Oh, I can't wait. In fact, why do I have to wait?"

Slade smiled. "I told you, I'm starving. We have reservations at 7:30, so get a move on."

I went into one of the bedrooms and stripped naked. Slade came into the bedroom and slid his arms around me. "You're serious about not making it to dinner, aren't you?"

"Join me in the shower," I said.

"If I do, then we seriously might not make it to dinner."

"So be it." I went into the bathroom, beckoning Slade with my finger.

With a grin, he stripped naked as well, and followed me into the bathroom.

There was an elegant jacuzzi that sat right in front of a wall of windows. It was truly tempting me, that jacuzzi, but I knew that Slade and I would be in that hot tub a little later. At the moment, Slade was hungry, and I was too. The plan was to get a shower, maybe fool around in the shower, and be at the restaurant in time for our reservation.

In the shower, Slade put some soap in his hands and soaped up my breasts. I felt the hot water rush over me, and what he was doing felt absolutely amazing.

"Mmmm," he said, "I know that we have reservations, but I really need to be inside of you. We're going to have to make this quick though."

I nodded my head and put my hands on the wall of the shower. I gasped as he took me right there, his commanding hands wrapped around my waist as the water cascaded down both of our bodies. He thrust in and out in an urgent fashion while I screamed out in ecstasy. He had his release and I could feel his cock throbbing inside of me.

Both of us took a few minutes to come down off of the high of the sex in the shower, and then he soaped up my hair and the rest of my body, taking special care to make sure that my nether-parts and inner folds were squeaky clean. Just the feeling of the sponge in those sensitive areas made me gasp, as I was still feeling the ecstasy of having his cock inside of me just a few minutes before.

The act of soaping me up apparently got him going as well, because I soon felt his cock grow hard and he entered me again. He took his time this time around, and I found myself coming again and again.

When we finally finished, he simply said, "that was amazing. And now I'm starving."

We managed to get to the restaurant in time for our reservation, and that was a good thing. The waiter brought out a bottle of wine when we got to the table and he recognized Slade and called him by name. "Mr. Bridgewell, it is very good to see you again," he said. "Are you in town for business or pleasure?"

"Pleasure this time. 100%. I'm going to a wedding in Montauk tomorrow."

"Yes, I heard about that. It's the daughter of Ryan Gallagher, right?"

"Right. Well, I think that we're ready to order," he said, motioning to me. I nodded my head. "She'll have the pumpkin mole soup and Bibb salad, no cheese, and I'll have the Walnut Sesame encrusted Cod."

"Very good sir," he said, and he disappeared.

"Hmmm," I said. "The waiter knows about my brother's wedding."

"That probably just means that it's something that high society has been talking about. I wouldn't be surprised, considering that your brother is starting to become famous in the art circles around here, and your new sister-in-law is the daughter of a fairly famous billionaire. I would be surprised if our waiter, whose name is John Wood, didn't know about this wedding."

I shook my head. "Who would have thought that Luke would be so successful at such a young age? I know that he has incredible talent, of course, so his success was kind of inevitable. But he's barely 22 years old, and he's taken the art world in New York by storm."

"I've seen his work, and I'm not surprised in the least. His art really does show a fresh and powerful voice. You should be proud of him."

"Oh, I am. He was a mess for awhile. Dalilah broke up with him because she wanted to help his art career. She married a man who was going to help Luke along by giving him a major showing at one of the large galleries in town. Of course, by the time I met Dalilah and reconnected with Luke, all of that drama had already blown over. He told me later, though, how devastated he was by her actions."

"Back up. Dalilah married somebody else?"

"Yes. His name is Nottingham, and he's a billionaire who lives here in town. He was obsessed with Dalilah, and he had offered Luke a showing at this huge gallery. That was before he found out that Dalilah and Luke were together. Once he found out that Dalilah was in love with Luke, he told her that he would pull Luke's show unless she married him, Nottingham. She married him, but only briefly, and she spent the next year or so trying to get away from him. So, marrying Nottingham was a mistake she made, but she made it for the right reasons."

"So she married Nottingham to save the person that she loved."

"Yes," I said pointedly. "And it was the absolute wrong choice for everyone involved." I knew that Slade would get the subtext of what I was saying to him. At least I hoped that he would.

Slade sighed. "I know what you're getting at, and believe me, I would do anything to avoid giving Charlotte just what she wants. What I'm not willing to do, though, is sacrifice you. If there's even a 1% chance that your life is in danger…" He shook his head and took a sip of his scotch and water, which had just arrived at the table, courtesy of John Wood the waiter. "As I said, though, I'm trying to figure out an alternative. I need to do that, though, before it's literally too late. If Charlotte decides to strike, she's going to do so without warning."

Our food arrived in short order, and I dug in with gusto. They certainly knew how to make delicious soup and salad, and, I had to admit, Slade's meal looked even more divine than mine did. But mine certainly was delicious in its own right.

"Slade, you have to figure something out. You might tell me that you can't see me in peril, but I'll tell you that I would literally rather die than see you married to that psychotic bitch. You know that once you're committed to her, there would be no leaving. She would kill you for sure, and me, too."

"Serena," he said to me, taking my hand. "If I do give Charlotte what she wants, it will have to be permanent, as you said. Believe me, doing something like that would be the very last resort. I'd only do that if I knew for sure that Charlotte was ready to jump. I'm in contact with her agent, who is giving me the latest news. I should know by the end of the weekend what's going on with her."

"Why don't we…" I was going to suggest that we cut the brakes on her car, but stopped short in asking him that. I realized that I was dead serious about that suggestion, and the mere thought that I really wanted that made me feel squeamish.

"Why don't we what?"

I shook my head. "Nothing. Let's talk about something else."

The evening wore on, and the wine flowed freely. By the time Slade and I we're ready to retire to our suite, I was feeling more than a little bit tipsy. I was looking forward to laying my head on that magnificent pillow on that amazing bed, and just falling asleep. Yet, I knew that Slade had other plans. Our quickie in the shower was something that was amazing, but I knew that the grand event was soon to come.

I knew that because I also knew that Slade had brought our toys on the trip.

We got back to the hotel room, and Slade went over to the grand piano. "What would you like to hear?" he asked me.

"I'm in the mood for a something light," I said. "Maybe some Bach or Mozart. As much as I love the Russian composers, their music is just a bit too dramatic for how I'm feeling this evening."

Slade smiled and launched into playing Beethoven's *Moonlight Sonata,* which actually was one of my favorite pieces. He played several more pieces that sounded like light chamber music by Bach and Mozart, and I went over to the bar and poured both of us a nightcap. I handed Slade one of the drinks as I sipped my own while I watched him intently. I eventually sat beside him, and he stopped playing.

"Hmmmm, maybe it's time that I played something else," he said, putting his arm around me.

"Maybe it is."

He slammed down the piano lid and hoisted me up on it. "Wait right here," he said.

He disappeared into one of the bedrooms, and I found myself getting wet with anticipation. I heard him humming in the other room and I touched myself while I waited for him. I put my finger on my clit and massaged it, and put one of my other fingers inside of myself. I needed to feel him on me, needed to feel his warm skin enveloping my own. We had this gorgeous suite, and we were going to make the most of it.

He came back out with a blindfold and two pairs of handcuffs. "Get undressed," he said.

I got up off the piano and slowly took off each layer of clothing. I took off my shoes and unbuckled my jeans, threw them off, and kicked them to the side. Next was my sweater and my bra. When I was completely naked, I stood before him, and he just stared at me appreciatively.

"You're like a work of art," he said. "Michelangelo wouldn't have been able to sculpt a more perfect form than your beautiful body."

I felt myself blushing, wondering if it was the fine scotch that was talking for him, or if he suddenly felt like opening up to me just a little bit more. "I could say the same about you."

He hoisted me up on the piano again, and blindfolded me. "Lay back," he ordered, "and lift up your legs."

I did as I was told, and he snapped the handcuffs, one on each hand, and attached each of my hands to my ankles. The cold steel cut into my skin, and I immediately felt a rush. I loved this feeling, of giving up total control. I didn't know what was coming, and that was what made the experience with Slade all the more enticing and exciting.

I was laying in that position, my bent legs attached to my wrists by the cold handcuffs, and I waited to see what he was going to do. I soon felt the sensation of something cold being spread on my vagina, and the sound of whipped cream being poured out of a container. It was the familiar *whoosh* that I always heard whenever somebody was indulging in that particular sweet treat.

I felt my clit stand to attention, as I knew that Slade was soon going to have his tongue and lips on that area. I wasn't disappointed, as he gently and firmly licked off the cream from my inner folds. His tongue danced around inside of me, and I moaned with pleasure.

"How does that feel?" he asked me.

"There are no words." And there weren't. There never were adequate words to describe how it felt when Slade made love to me. It just seemed sometimes that he put me onto a different planet. That was how amazing of a lover he was.

He caressed my stomach, and then started to kiss it, while his hands moved deftly to my breasts. He secured clamps on each of my nipples, and the sweet pain of these clamps sent wave after wave of adrenaline coursing throughout my body. I moaned a little, reveling in the pain of the clamps, which mixed with the absolute pleasure of his touch. I tried to move my legs, which was only instinctive, but I couldn't move them at all. That fact sent another wave of pleasurable release throughout my body, as I realized, anew, that I was helpless. I was at his mercy, and I loved it.

He positioned himself so that he was halfway on top of me on the piano, and I heard him unbuckle his pants. The scent of sweet strawberries permeated the air, and I opened my mouth, wanting to taste one. I soon had a strawberry in my mouth, its sweetness working its way through every taste bud. I chewed it slowly, and then another strawberry was in my mouth, and one more after that.

Then I felt the unmistakable sensation of anal beads working their way through my ass. As one lubed bead after another went into my opening, I felt the exquisite sensation of being filled with each of the beads. I gasped when he finally got the last bead inserted, and then, in one smooth move, he took out the beads. I clenched the inner walls of my nether-parts, which were exploding as the beads came out. I cried out in sweet release, and Slade immediately put a ball-gag on me. "Relax," he said, "enjoy yourself, but not too much. Your orgasm belong to me, and you can't experience one until I say that you can."

I nodded my head in assent, and tried to talk to myself. I silently thought in my head *calm down, calm down. What he's doing is amazing, but you belong to him, and you will do as he says.* Or suffer the consequences, I thought.

Then he entered me, and I felt that my inner folds and clit were absolutely on fire. They were filled with blood and so sensitive that I wanted so badly to scream, but I couldn't because of the gag. He was going in deep, hitting my G-spot again and again while I was trussed up on that piano, unable to move. I moved my head from side to side, desperately trying to control myself, but finding it difficult.

His strong hands moved from my waist to my breasts, and his lips grazed my nipples lightly. He kissed my neck and shoulders while he drove into me with a force that he hadn't displayed before. He took my ball gag off, so I was able to scream out loud, and I did, because I had yet another earth-shattering orgasm. Then he came inside of me with a force that made me want to split in two.

He lay on top of me, his breathing hard and his heart beating out of his chest. We both were sweating, and my own heart was beating like it never had before. He silently unlocked the handcuffs on my wrists and ankles and brought me off the piano. My legs were unsteady because of the powerful release I just had, and I collapsed into his arms.

He laughed as he caught me. "Let's go to bed," he said. "We're going to have a long day tomorrow, and I want to be on my best behavior in front of your family."

I smiled as I realized how badly he wanted to impress my father, brothers, sisters and extended family. He looked almost shy when he talked about being on his best behavior, and I thought that he was blushing just a little.

Slade, blushing? What was the world coming to?

Chapter Sixteen

The next day, the limo came around to take us to Montauk. The rehearsal dinner was that evening at a country club there. As much as I was looking forward to this – and I really was – I couldn't shake off the undercurrent of nerves that seemed to permeate every cell of my body. I hated being this jumpy, but I couldn't help it. Ever since Slade had his talk with me about Charlotte and the fact that she seemed like she was ready to call off her deal with him, I had been on pins and needles.

I looked out the window of the limo, and Slade put his hand on my leg. "Hey," he said. "I think that I know how to make you feel less nervous." His hand crawled further up my leg, and he shut the barrier between us and the driver. "You can't go to the rehearsal dinner looking like you've seen a ghost."

I have seen a ghost, and that ghost is me. In spite of myself, though, I smiled at Slade, and my smile was genuine. "Slade," I said, "what did you have in mind?"

"What did you think that I had in mind?" He smiled

back, but I could see the devilish glint in his eye. "Have you ever fucked in a limo before?"

I thought back. The only other time that I had been alone with a man in a limo, besides Slade, was prom night. I wasn't about to sleep with HarrySl, who was my prom date for the evening. For one, I think that he lived up to his name, because he had a really hairy back. For another, that prom happened too close to my rape, and I was always walking around half-there after that incident. I had not yet learned to channel my rage into underground sex clubs, and I wasn't feeling at all amorous with anyone.

It really wasn't until I had met Slade that I started to feel whole again. I was able to integrate all those pieces of me that had scared me before – my need for pain, my need to be controlled in bed, and my need to be dominated – in my relationship with Slade, and I knew that I couldn't lose him. I knew how rare it was to find a kindred soul, and Slade was definitely that. "I can't say that I've ever fucked in a limo before, but, believe me, I'm anxious to try."

"Well, we have about three hours until we hit Montauk," he said. "Let's make every single one of those minutes count, shall we?"

Slade put the barrier up between us and the limo driver, and then he brought one of my legs onto his lap, and his strong and firm hand started to make its way up my thigh. I started to quake a little, feeling his commanding touch on my leg. Then he pinched my inner thigh hard. His hand made its way further up my thigh and was soon on my clit, rubbing it through my thong underwear. He tickled my clit, then one of his fingers was inside of me. I could feel my breathing coming faster and faster as one finger, then two, gently rubbed inside of me.

"You're so wet," he whispered, and then commanded

me to lie on my stomach. I obeyed and Slade hiked up my skirt. His hands were on my bare ass, and he spanked my bare cheek hard with his hand. Then he rubbed my cheeks and stroked them lightly with one of his hands, with his other hand stroking my inner thigh, which moved up to my clit. His tongue soon made its way to my clit, and I moaned.

"Lie on your back," he commanded, and I turned over so that I was lying on my back. He then removed my skirt, and he rubbed his hands on my waist, making its way underneath my top. He rubbed my breasts over my bra while he fingered my clit. With one flick of his finger, my bra was undone and I felt my breasts spilling out. He unbuttoned my shirt, and his mouth was on one of my nipples. He gently ran his tongue around the nipple, then around the rest of my breast. He did the same with my other breast while his fingers worked my clit the entire time he was doing this.

His mouth made its way up to my neck, and then he started to kiss me passionately on the lips. His hand was still on my breast, and his other hand was still exploring inside of me. He was still fully clothed, but he removed his jacket, and unbuttoned his dress shirt. I lost my breath, as I always did, as I examined his beautiful body. He was one of the most beautiful men I had ever seen. His beauty to me was almost intoxicating. I would never get tired of seeing his rippling muscles, his gorgeous face and enormous manhood.

He plunged his fingers deep inside of me, and he lay me down on the seat and his cock made its way slowly inside of me. He filled me up, inch by inch, while my legs were wrapped around his back. He started to finger my ass as his enormous manhood was slipping in and out. I was quaking underneath, and a powerful sensation of pleasure overcame me, and my entire body started to writhe under-neath him.

"Go ahead and scream, Serena. I know you want to," he said, as he moved in and out of me rhythmically. I started to moan, then screamed out wildly. I couldn't keep it in any longer. I felt the powerful release building inside me, the feeling that my entire body was on fire, and that the fire needed to be quenched by Slade's touch.

He continued to move in and out of me, while I screamed out loud. I had never felt so alive as I did right at that moment.

Then he flipped me on my stomach, and his finger was just inside my rear end. He put some kind of lubricant on the edge, and his fingers slipped inside of me. Then he was on top of me. His manhood was on the edge of my rear opening, and he gently and slowly entered me. As before, when we did this, the pain started out as unbearable while he plunged his cock deeper and deeper inside my butt, and then he spanked one of my cheeks. His manhood plunged even deeper inside of me, and it felt like it was ripping up my insides. I squeezed my eyes shut tight, trying to will away the pain, knowing that it was going to start feeling amazing.

Out of nowhere, the extreme pain turned into extreme pleasure. My body was flooded with pleasurable sensations as he stroked in and out of my ass. His lips were on my neck, and his hands were on my breasts. He squeezed each one of my nipples as he pounded me harder and harder. I felt the overwhelming urge to scream out in pleasure and pain, as each of these sensations were overtaking my body. These twin sensations were indistinguishable from one another at this point. They were one and same, and each was as powerful as the other. I finally screamed out as I released an earth-shattering orgasm. My breathing started coming faster and faster, and my body shook underneath him.

Then, he stopped pounding me. He lay down on top of me, breathing heavily. His hand was in my hair, and he started pulling it lightly. Then he flipped me over on my back and kissed me gently. I smiled at his tender touch, which conveyed to me things that couldn't be put into words. His touch told me how much I meant to him, and how much he was in love with me. His eyes, as they looked into mine, expressed the same things.

I sighed as I put on my clothes and he did the same, both of us without a word.

There were no words for how we both were feeling, which is why there was the silence. But it was understood, and it was beautiful.

Chapter Seventeen

We finally arrived in Montauk and made our way to the country club. This was a quaint little town, much less crowded than many of the other Hampton area hot spots and was practically deserted in the fall. Well, it wasn't deserted, but it was certainly less crowded. Shops lined the streets, and there were a few people milling about in the coffee shops and boutiques.

The Montauk Yacht Club was located on the water and was enormous. It consisted of about ten different buildings, all with red roofs, and a structure in the middle that resembled a light house. This was apparently the place where the well-heeled Hamptonians would gather to watch boat races and the like. Today, there weren't any boat races, but there were still a lot of people. Most of them were dressed up, and I assumed that they were coming to this rehearsal dinner as well.

We were led into a ballroom where waiters with black ties were serving drinks and hors d'oeuvres on shiny platters. I was offered a glass of champagne by one of them, and I

took it, as did Slade. Another waiter came around with a tray of shrimp cocktail and some veggies and dip. I took the veggies and Slade took some shrimp. We both looked around the place, which was filling up rapidly.

At the front of the room was Ryan. This was Dalilah's father, and, even though he was at least fifty, he was still devastatingly handsome. I imagined that Slade would look like Ryan when he got to be that age. His thick dark hair was greying only slightly at the temples, and his face was unlined. He had a huge smile on his face as he greeted everyone who came up to him.

Next to him was Iris, who was his wife. She, too, didn't look her age, although she wasn't quite as beautiful as her husband. Her hair had lightened considerably over the years, judging from the pictures of her when she was a young girl. She used to have flaming hair, but it had since faded to a pale ginger. She was dressed in a sleek blue number, while Ryan had on a tuxedo and black tie. Her hair was swooped up on her head, and she looked considerably less comfortable with this crowd than did Ryan.

I knew why. She came from a working-class background. Dalilah had explained to me that her mother was never quite comfortable with the high-society types, but was always much more comfortable with the help. Indeed, she seemed much more relaxed when she was talking to the cater waiters and the bartenders than she did speaking with some of the guests. I did a quick perusal of the cars that were out in the parking lot, and saw quite a few Lamborghinis, Bentleys and Rolls-Royces out there. That told me all that I needed to know about this crowd, and I knew why Iris looked like she wanted to be anywhere but here.

I often felt the same way whenever I was around the muckety-mucks. I might have been around them, but I

wasn't one of them, and I never would be. I was the daughter of a fisherman, and that was who I was under the "costume" that I showed to the world. Iris was probably the same, while Ryan was to the manor born. I could tell, just in their demeanor, who they really were inside.

I went over to them to greet them and tell them congratulations.

"Thank you," Iris said, looking around. "I never thought that I'd take part in a wedding quite like this one. When Ryan and I got married, it was in his backyard, and we had Stroud's chicken to serve to our guests. Here we are at the fancy-schmancy yacht club, and I really have to pee," she said in a low voice. Her hand was on my shoulder, as if she were telling me a great big secret. "And I don't think that I can leave until I have greeted all the guests."

I had to laugh when Iris' conspiratorial words and tone told me exactly why she was looking so uncomfortable. "You better go. When nature calls, it won't be denied."

She looked aecross the room with a worried expression on her face. She turned to her husband, who was busy chatting with Slade.

"Go," Ryan said, gesturing to the restroom that was all the way across the ballroom. "I'll hold down the fort. But don't take too long."

At that, Iris walked purposefully across the room and disappeared. Ryan looked at me and smiled. "Serena, I can't tell you how happy I am to see you. You're the first one of your family to arrive. I think that Christopher is stuck in traffic, as he's coming from the city, and your father and stepmother will be here any minute. I've also heard from Mark and Amy, and they're on their way as well."

"That's good to hear," I said, although I felt vaguely apprehensive about seeing my family. They hated me, or

they did hate me, for so many years. Luke finally got them to turn around and see me for who I was, and that meant that they hated me a bit less. But Amy had always judged me, and so did Mark. They were both too straight-laced for their own damned good. Chris had judged me much less, probably because his life was filled with drama, drugs and jail stints. He really had no room to judge me. And Luke was always so laid-back. He was therefore the easiest to win over.

There was little love lost between myself and my father, but I had always hoped to change that as well.

Ryan smiled, big, and I was briefly mesmerized. He certainly had a smile that would light up any room. I looked over at Slade and again thought that Slade was going to age like this man – Ryan just kept getting better-looking with every year.

Ryan put his hand on my shoulder. "Now, you and Slade are at that table over there," he said, pointing to a table that had red roses as its centerpiece. It was then that I noticed that every table had a different bouquet of flowers in the middle. Some of the tables had tulips in different colors, and others had roses in all different shades. Still others had bouquets of different wild flowers and one table had a centerpiece with birds of paradise, the tropical flower that had a magnificent orange color and had a very unusual bud. "You're going to be seated with a United States Senator and a CEO of a multimillion dollar hedge fund." He shook his head. "I know what you're thinking, but I swear, this will be a fun evening."

I raised my eyebrows at Slade, who smiled at me. "Don't worry, I got this," he said, as we left Ryan and headed to our table. "I know how you hate the men in the monkey suits."

I smiled at Slade. He did know me so well, even if we

had only been together for less than a year. "Now, how did you know that?"

"I remember that party that I had for the ASPCA full of important people, right when you and I first met. You looked like somebody who would have rather been sitting in front of a firing squad than being around all those people. Don't worry, you're not alone."

We sat down and Slade didn't even have to introduce himself. The two men at our table, the Senator and the CEO, already knew him. They were like old friends.

"Slade, my man, what are you doing here?" asked an older gentleman with white hair and a large bald spot. He was dressed in a high-dollar suit, and, next to him, was a 40-something woman who looked like she was a former super-model. She was in better shape than somebody half her age, and, with her light hazel eyes, olive skin, and dark hair, she was truly a beautiful woman. She wore an off the shoulder black number and daintily sipped a glass of champagne.

The two men embraced and we sat down. "Serena, this is Senator Hodges. He's from the great state of New York. Senator Hodges, this is my significant other, Serena Roberts. She's the sister of the groom, Luke."

"Good to meet you, Serena. This is my wife, Leda," he said, putting his arm around the gorgeous woman. "Leda, this is Slade Bridgewell, but you probably already know that, and Serena Roberts."

Leda smiled warmly and held out her hand for Slade to shake and then did the same for me. "Nice to meet you both."

We made some small talk before being greeted by another man that came over to Slade. He put his hand on Slade's shoulder. "Slade, you bastard. I'm still waiting for your phone call about getting Alecta approved." This man was middle-aged and handsome. He was smiling as he was talking, so I had to assume that he was joking around with Slade.

Slade stood up and embraced the man. "Alex, what are you up to these days? Sorry I didn't get back with you about that drug, but, as you know, I've been a bit preoccupied these days."

"I know. I'm just busting you. Congratulations on beating that murder charge, by the way." He looked over at me. "She with you?"

"Yes. Serena, this is Alex Moore. Alex is the CEO of a biotech company in Palo Alto."

We shook hands and Slade turned to him. "What brings you clear across the country like this?"

"I'm good friends with Ryan. I do a lot of work and giving to his charity, because protecting animal rights is a big passion of mine." He looked around. "This place looks like a 'who's-who' of the high society types."

Slade looked around too. "Sure does." Then he turned to me. "Don't worry, Serena. I won't be schmoozing tonight. I'll stick by your side."

"Slade, you don't have to. If this event is going to be like a networking opportunity for you, then I say go for it. I have to reconnect with my family anyhow."

Slade just shrugged his shoulders and Alex sat down next to him. "What a happy coincidence, we're at the same table," Alex said with a smile. "My girlfriend is around here somewhere. She's always ditching me. She's kind of a climber."

"Aren't they all?" Slade asked. Then he looked over at me. "Except Serena. She's as far from a climber as you can get."

Alex just rolled his eyes and shook his head. Then he bent down to say something private to Slade, and Slade just nodded his head and looked sympathetic.

I looked around the room, trying to see if anybody from my family had show up. A few minutes later, I saw Chris. He was standing in a group of people, trying to look interested, but I knew better. He was probably bored to tears. He clearly looked like he wanted to have a guitar in his hand, and he probably did. His guitar was like his crutch, I thought ruefully. Chris, out of all of my family, had the most problems dealing with my mother's death. It was obvious why he had so many issues with it. He saw our mother die, lying dead in a pool of her own blood, shot and killed while trying to protect him. Add to that the mere fact that he was involved in a mass shooting, and he would have died himself if the gunman hadn't run out of bullets, and you had a perfect storm for poor Chris.

I went over to him and embraced him. He looked almost startled, but he was soon hugging me back. "Sis, it's good to see you," he said. He sounded sincere, and I felt a bit more positive.

"Good to see you too." I took a look at him. His hair was a bit long, just past his shoulders, but he had it in a ponytail, so it didn't look too bad. He looked like he had been working out. I always remembered him as being skinny, but he was really looking muscular. With his hazel-green eyes, chiseled features and a new muscular frame, Chris was really a great-looking guy, I thought, even better looking than his identical twin, Mark. I guess the reason why he seemed better-looking to me than Mark was that Mark could be such a straight-laced douchebag sometimes. Chris, on the other hand, was sensitive and kind and creative. He had a lot of darkness in his life, but he channeled it into his music these days, instead of into drugs like he did in his youth. And he was completely non-judgmental. Basically, for Chris, if you're not hurting other people, you're good.

He looked around the room nervously. "I never thought Luke would be involved in a shindig like this."

"Me neither. Then again, who would have ever thought that Luke would be taking the art world by storm at such a young age."

Chris smiled a shy smile. "It was inevitable, wasn't it? After all, his soon-to-be-wife was the one who put Luke on the map. Her and that cray-cray Nottingham."

"We won't speak of that," I said as I sipped my drink. "That's all behind us."

"Yeah. Anyhow, I don't know if you heard or not. Probably not, but my band was just signed to Liam Gallagher's record label. I'm totally stoked about that, because he's discovered some huge names. I just hope that Metronics is the next big name to come out of his label. We go into the studio next week to record some demos."

I hugged him. "That's great! See, I knew that you'd be signed. And you're right – Liam has discovered some major names along the way. I've heard your music, and I think that you guys have the stuff to make it big." Chris' band fused some good ole' fashioned grunge sound with some other influences, including Ska, Punk and even some MoTown funk. It was a sound that was fresh and new, yet one that I could imagine emerging as huge in the next few years. Who knows? Maybe Metronics would be the Nirvana of grunge fusion and would really put that particular genre on the map.

"Here's hoping," he said, lifting his glass. I lifted my own and clinked it with his.

He smiled. "Dalilah might be responsible for my success as well. After all, Liam is her cousin, and she introduced me to him. Liam has also sold a few of Luke's songs that he has written, and they're going to be recorded by some major artists. Luke really struck gold when he met that girl."

"He did strike gold, and not just because Dalilah has helped you and Luke in your careers. She's really an awesome girl, too."

Chris smiled. "Yeah. Too bad I don't have my awesome girl tonight."

I wasn't aware that Chris had been seeing anybody. Last I heard, he had dumped his lady love because she didn't support his dreams. "Who are you seeing?"

"Nobody. That's why I don't have an awesome girl here tonight."

I lowered my voice. "Well, sometimes it happens when you least expect it. That's what happened with Slade and me."

"I guess. Anyhow, did you have a chance to meet your two new step-sisters? I think that they're around here somewhere."

"I don't think that I would recognize them even if I did see them. Where are they?"

He motioned over to a girl who was standing in the corner. She clearly knew nobody, and, like the rest of my family, including me, she looked like she wanted to be anywhere else but here. "That's Bailey," he said. She was just how I had described her to Slade, having seen pictures of her before. Her hair was a dark shade of purple, and was really quite beautiful. She had a nose ring and a sullen expression. She turned her back to us unveiling a backless gown that showed off an enormous tattoo.

Next to Bailey was apparently Rayanne. She looked

exactly like Bailey, except her hair was dark and looked to be her natural color, and she had on a good deal less makeup than her twin sister. She, too, had on a backless gown, but her back didn't have a single mark on it.

Both girls were gorgeous.

I went over to talk to them. "Hello, I'm Serena," I said, extending my right hand to the two girls. "I guess I'm your step-sister." It seemed weird to be introducing myself in that way. I was 28 years old and I never imagined that I would be getting a new stepsister, let alone two new stepsisters.

Rayanne smiled and gave me a hug. "I would say welcome to the family, but I guess that goes both ways."

Bailey, for her part, also came over and gave me a hug, albeit much more reluctantly than Rayanne. "Yay," she said without enthusiasm. "I'm so excited." She sounded anything but excited, however. She looked around the room. "I really need a drink or some pot. I can't imagine getting through this evening sober."

I was amused that Bailey seemed to be so open.

Rayanne gave a little nudge to Bailey, who rolled her eyes back at her sister. "What? Tell me that you're not thinking the exact same thing."

"Of course I am, but that's just because we don't really know anyone here. And there aren't any hot guys here just yet, except for our new stepbrother Chris, of course." Then she spied Slade across the room. "And that guy right there," she said, pointing at Slade. "But he's with you, isn't he?"

"Yes, he is."

Bailey kind of threw her hands up in a gesture of frustration. "Well, there you go. The one hot guy, besides the one that we're stuck being related to, is taken."

"Story of our life," Rayanne said with a laugh. "Anyhow, Serena, it's great to meet you." Then she looked over at Slade a little more closely. "Oh, I know where I've seen him. I was thinking he looked familiar. He's the hot rich dude who was up for murder, isn't he? He just got the charges dropped though, right?"

"You got it," I said. "It was a crazy thing, and it's not over yet."

Rayanne nodded her head knowingly. "Right. It seems that he gets over that murder thing, and gets right back into another charge. Sucks to be him, doesn't it?"

I laughed. "Oh, you don't know the half of it." If only Rayanne knew about crazy Charlotte, she would really know just how much it sucked to be Slade.

"Maybe you can tell me sometime," she said. Then she looked towards the entrance of the ballroom, where Mark was walking in through the door. She sighed. "Mark. Goddamn, our stepbrothers are hot."

Indeed, Mark was looking particularly "hot" that evening. He was dressed in a suit that looked tailored, and his dark hair was cut short. He had just a hint of a goatee growing on his face, and, like Chris, it looked like he had been making an effort at working out.

I felt badly about not being in touch with Mark. After all, he and I lived in the same city. He was studying marine biology at the University of California-San Diego. Yet, I had lived in San Diego for almost a year, and I had never once called him to meet me for lunch or for a drink.

Mark approached us, and, to my huge surprise, he put his arm around me. "Serena, you made it," he said. "I should have asked if you wanted to travel with me. I actually drove here, across the country, because I wanted to see America." He smiled. "But I understand that you took a private plane here, and if you'd like to offer me a ride back, I won't say no."

I cocked my head and studied him. It was strange that he was being so friendly, but it was also heartening. "I'd love for you to ride back with us, but where would you put your car?"

"I need to sell it anyhow. It's a hoopdie."

"Then sure, sell it and ride back with us. I think that we're leaving on Monday morning, though. You'll have to miss your Monday classes."

He shrugged. "So be it. The professors know that I'm here this weekend, anyhow, so that won't be such a huge deal."

Truth be told, I was actually looking forward to the plane ride back with Mark. I was eager to find out any of the gossip that was happening while I was away and not in touch with the rest of the family. I also really wanted to find out how my siblings and father were feeling about me these days.

Mark then gave Bailey and Rayanne a big hug. I thought that Rayanne blushed a tiny bit, and I had to smile. She had a little crush, that much was sure. I could recognize it anywhere. I had a crush on my first cousin when we were growing up, and I'm sure that my face looked just like Rayanne's did in that moment.

For her part, Bailey looked as disinterested in Mark as she did the entire affair.

My father arrived with his new wife, and he looked dapper and happy. He also seemed to want to let bygones be bygones, because he gave me a big hug and told me that he was thrilled to see me. Caroline, his new wife, was dressed in a gorgeous gown that was perfect for the mother of the groom. Her naturally dark hair was cropped short and had streaks of auburn running through it. She must have been in her fifties, but you would never know it by looking at her, because she was super-fit.

Next to arrive were Amy, her husband, and her new baby, whose name was Addison. She was just a bit more standoffish, but I put her off-guard with a big hug, and she looked astonished and awkward at the same time. "Serena," she said, "um, I'm glad that you could come."

I smiled and put my arm around her. "Of course. I wouldn't miss this for the world." I looked at her baby, who was smiling right at me. "Can I hold her?"

"Of course," she said, handing me the infant. "You're her aunt."

The docile child smiled at me and reached a chubby hand towards my face. I laughed a little and touched her nose. "Beautiful baby," I said.

"She is." Amy seemed to genuinely be happy to see me, and that heartened me. "I need to find Mark," she said. "I have to tell him something. But I'll find you later, huh?"

I nodded my head and handed her back Addison, who started to cry. Amy rolled her eyes. "Of course, once I get her back, she starts to fuss. But it was nice to see you, Serena. Don't be a stranger, okay?"

"I won't."

Next, I spotted Nick and Scotty, who were Dalilah's godparents. Nick was Ryan's best friend from the time that they were kids, and was a nice guy. He, just like Ryan, looked amazing. He was a natural blonde, and his hair wasn't getting grey at all. He was still fit and trim, and his gorgeous wife, Scotty, was in her forties and didn't look a day over 25. I approached them and shook both of their hands.

"Serena," Nick said, giving me a big hug. "It's good to see you."

Scotty also gave me a hug. "You look beautiful," she said to me.

"I'd say the same about you. My god, girl, you just don't age."

She rolled her eyes. "Yeah, right. I wish. But thank you so much for saying that."

"Where are the kids?"

"They'll be along a bit later. You know how twenty-somethings are. They like to be fashionably late, and our kids are no different."

I scanned the room and found Slade mesmerized in conversation with the Senator. After a few minutes, though, I saw him surveying the room, and I thought that maybe he was looking for me. "Would you excuse me," I said to Nick and Scotty. "I think that my boyfriend needs me."

After talking to everyone a few minutes more, I headed back to our table.

"Senator Hodges is very helpful for me," Slade said in a low voice when I got back to the table. "He has some sway with the FDA, so hopefully the approval of one of my drugs will be on the fast track. It's a drug that will hopefully be another huge hit, so the faster it gets to market, the better off we will be."

"What drug are you talking about?"

"The marijuana pill. Also, Senator Hodges has been on the forefront in removing marijuana from the Schedule One list. It's going to be difficult mass-marketing this pill when marijuana is still not only illegal on the federal level, but also considered to be one of the most dangerous drugs there is by the federal government. As it is, the marijuana pill is only going to be available in the states where the drug is legal, of course. But I think that it can do extremely well for people who can't tolerate smoking it and don't like edibles because they take too long and are too unpredictable. This pill might also open up the market, in general, once people start to realize how much good it's going to do."

"Well, good luck with that," I said to him, squeezing his knee.

He smiled. "How are your brother and your new sisters-in-law?"

"They all seem to be doing fine. Mark would like to ride back with us to San Diego, if that's okay. He drove here, but he wants to sell his car anyhow. Would that be okay?"

"The more the merrier."

I kissed him on the cheek. "I knew that you would say that."

"Of course. I'm all for you taking any chance you can to reconnect with your family. I know how much you miss them and regret the years that you were estranged."

I couldn't help but stare at Slade's gorgeous face. I realized that I loved him more than I thought it was possible to love another human being. He was always so kind and loving and good to me. Then I closed my eyes, and didn't try to tune into his vibrations or anyone else's. I was searching within myself for answers to my future with Slade. There was still so much against it. I needed to continue to keep a wall up, because if I didn't, I was surely going to be hurt. Or worse. Charlotte had plans for me, of that I was sure.

Just then, the wedding party was coming through the door. Actually, there wasn't really a wedding party, since Dalilah and Luke apparently decided not to have attendants. So, it was really just the happy couple. Everyone stood and applauded as they took their seats at the head table. Also seated at this table were Ryan, Iris, my father, and his new wife, Carolyn. They sat down, and then the waiters started to bring around the food in covered dishes. Everyone dined on steak and lobster with risotto, while I was served a scrumptious vegetable lasagna with cashew cheese. It was evident that Ryan had pulled out all the stops for this affair, and why shouldn't he? His only child was getting married.

Dalilah looked every inch the gorgeous, blushing bride. Another gorgeous woman had little Olivia in her arms, and she handed the child to Dalilah, who cradled her while she ate her dinner. Luke had his arm protectively around his wife-to-be, and I thought that I had never seen him so happy in my life.

The food was delicious, and, to my surprise, I found myself actually enjoying talking with Senator Hodges and Alex Moore about the issues. I was always interested in talking policy to powerful people, and Senator Hodges was knowledgeable about some of my key issues. Alex entertained us with unusual stories that concerned the area of bio-ethics, which was always a controversial one.

After everyone was done eating, we were entertained by a slide-show showing pictures of both Dalilah and Luke as they were growing up. Dalilah was shown playing soccer, reading a difficult book at a very young age, and going to various parties around the world. Her artwork was also displayed on the screen, and I was astounded by how mature it was, even though she did her best work when she was only 11 years old. Dalilah appeared, through the photo montage, to be a popular girl who even went through her own punk phase at one time. Some of the pictures showed her hair dyed various shades of the rainbow, as she looked at the camera with a sullen expression.

Luke's montage was similar, yet strikingly dissimilar in many ways. There were no photos of Luke blowing out candles with the Alps in the background, as there were with Dalilah. Luke had never even been overseas before he met Dalilah. In these photos, he was fishing with our dad, rough-housing with various friends, and, in some of the most poignant photos, was hugging our mother. I couldn't help but feel a lump in my throat as I looked at those particular photos, for Luke and my mom looked extremely happy. There was mom and a 2-year-old Luke at Macy's for the Thanksgiving Parade. There they were at an amusement park, with Luke looking like he wanted to puke and mom smiling broadly. They were part of the family photos that were taken while we camped. And on and on.

The lights finally came on and Dalilah addressed the crowd. "I'd like to thank everyone for coming tonight. Tomorrow is going to be just an incredible experience, and it's going to be even more special because you will all be there too. Luke and I are just incredibly happy to have so much love, light and warmth surrounding us."

Luke stood up, and I knew that he wasn't much of a public speaker. He looked kind of embarrassed to be speaking to such a large crowd of people, but he managed a few words. "You guys rock," he said. "Dalilah and I are completely excited to start our lives together, and I know that a few of you traveled across the country to be here, so thanks."

Everyone applauded again, and I looked over at Slade. I was thinking how nice it would be if the two of us were addressing a crowd in our near future. He was looking at me, and, when I closed my eyes, I felt the love coming from him. I felt hope. Hope was emanating from every one of his pores. Yet, underlying all the positive emotions I was feeling from him, I also distinctly felt a sense of worry. I knew why – he was worried that he and I weren't going to get our happy ending. He was still trying to figure out the quagmire that was Charlotte, and, thus far, neither of us had a good plan to deal with her.

Slade put his arm around me and whispered "I thought that coming here would freak me out just a bit, although I didn't tell you that. But I'm actually feeling inspired by these two. Maybe a happy ending isn't so much out of the question for you and me."

I felt the tingles when he said that to me, and, just for a moment, I started to feel my own brand of hope. There were obstacles in front of Slade and me and they were enormous. But were they insurmountable? Were the obstacles in the way of Dalilah and Luke insurmountable? They seemed to be for the longest time, but they overcame them. Slade and I would overcome ours as well. We had to.

Dessert came around and the wine was flowing freely. After dessert was served, everyone got up and mingled about, and a band appeared and set up. They soon were playing a mix of dance tunes and some alternative rock, and I wondered how the actual reception was going to go. This rehearsal dinner seemed more like a party than a dinner, but, then again, the reception was going to be on the beach, so it was probably going to be one helluva time.

By the time the evening came to a close, I was thoroughly convinced that Slade and I were going to beat the odds. We would. Just like couples did, all over the world. It was harder for Slade and me, just because not everyone had a psycho involved who wanted them dead, but we were still going to make it.

We just had to.

Chapter Eighteen

The next day was the actual wedding, and, I had to admit, Mother Nature was being completely cooperative. It was October, so the weather was always going to be questionable. Yet the day turned out to be unseasonably warm, for Indian Summer had apparently rolled in while nobody was looking. Even on the beach, people were able to wear their suits and dresses without jackets or hats, and Dalilah, in her sleeveless and backless white dress, looked gorgeous and not at all shivering. Still, the evening was bound to be a bit cool, even if the daytime was warm, so I hoped that they had plenty of heat lamps under the tents that were set up throughout the sandy beach.

Dalilah made her way to the altar, with Ryan next to her, his arm interlocking with hers. I couldn't help but think that I hadn't seen two more beautiful people in my entire life than those two. Dalilah actually looked happier than I had ever seen her. And my brother looked like he just won the lottery. That actually was accurate, because marrying Dalilah was like winning the lottery.

She got to the altar, and she actually seemed just a bit nervous. The preacher was talking about love, commitment and sticking things out through thick and thin, and Luke and Dalilah were just standing there, holding hands and gazing into each other's eyes. When Luke started to talk, his voice cracked a little, and I thought, for just a second, that he was holding back tears. He might have been, although I confess that I had never seen him cry. Not even after our mother was killed. He was a stoic sort, although very good-natured.

Dalilah's turn came and she recited a beautiful poem that she said she created herself. As she spoke, I thought that Dalilah had a special talent for words, almost as great as her talent for the canvas.

While the ceremony was carrying on, Slade was gripping my hand tightly. He was rubbing his thumb on the crease between my own thumb and index finger. "What are you thinking?" he whispered to me.

I shrugged my shoulders, not wanting to tell him what I was really thinking. I was thinking that I wanted Slade and me to be at the altar sometime in the near future. But I couldn't tell him that. I was always getting an odd vibe from him that prevented me from really telling him that I saw forever with him. "Just that I think I've never seen two happier people in my life."

Slade smiled. "I was thinking the exact same thing."

At some point, the preacher told Luke to "kiss the bride," and he did, giving her a long, long kiss. Then everybody started to clap and throw rose petals as the two practically sprinted down the aisle. They were laughing, and everybody else started to laugh as well. There was such a feeling of love and light in this space, and it wasn't just that the day was warm and sunny, and the ocean was just feet away. It was that Luke and Dalilah just spread happiness throughout the crowd.

We all followed them to the reception, which was also on the beach, in tents that were set up throughout. In the tents, there was good alcohol flowing freely, and a smorgasbord of rich food. Lobsters, filet mignons, different salads, tropical fruits, and various side dishes were warming up in pans. There was a band in each of the tents, and each band was playing a different style of music. One was playing standards, another was playing dance music, another was playing show tunes, another was playing alternative rock, and yet another was playing classical. Slade and I wandered around the tents, socializing with people as we went, and drinking lots of champagne.

Slade and I waited until the crowd around the couple had thinned out, and we approached them. I gave them both a hug. "Kid, you did it," I said to Luke. "After what you guys went through, I was skeptical, but you did it. Congratulations."

Luke was smiling, big. "Of course we did it. There was never a doubt in my mind. Not when Dalilah was trapped in that hell of a marriage with that creep, and not when all those horrible things happened to us. I never lost faith."

Dalilah chimed in. "I was never as sure as Luke was that we would be endgame, but I always hoped that we would be." She whispered to me. "If I believed in the concept of soul mates, I would say that I found mine."

I looked over at Slade. "I think that I did too."

She smiled and shook Slade's hand daintily. Slade took her hand and then embraced her in a hug. She almost blushed when he did that. Most women did blush around Slade, I thought. He just had that effect on almost everyone.

The happy couple had the first dance, and then

everyone joined in. As Louis Armstrong sang about a wonderful world, Slade held me tight against him. I put my head on this chest, and wrapped both my arms around him. He hummed the song in my ear, and I felt like I was going to melt in a pool right there on the floor.

The night went on like that. As evening fell, the heat lamps came on, and everyone started to get at least slightly tipsy. Slade and I danced all night, going from one tent to another, and generally feeling the love surround us. There wasn't anything in that evening but happiness. Charlotte and her evil plan felt like it was a zillion miles away.

Of course, I knew that this was a feeling that I had that evening, and I was fairly certain that it was a moment that was fleeting, as all moments are. A course correction was coming soon, and it wasn't going to be stopped.

Of that, I was sure.

Chapter Nineteen

We spent the rest of the weekend exploring old haunts and, on Monday, we met Mark at the airport. He was dressed casually in jeans and a sweater, and he had his luggage ready to go. "I sold my car," he said. "And I'm ready to get back."

"As we all are," I said, glancing at Slade. I felt a well of nervous energy coming to the surface, and I tried to tamp it down. The weekend had been so perfect, magical even, that the coming reality in San Diego was going to be even more difficult to face. That was always the problem with vacations in general – there was bound to be a post-vacation letdown, no matter what happened.

We all boarded Slade's plane, and, for the first few minutes, I thought that the ride back was going to be awkward. I never had much to say to Mark. Out of all my brothers, he was the one that I felt bonded to the least. It was just that he always seemed to be just a bit uptight and judgmental. He was an identical twin to Chris, and they couldn't be more different.

To my surprise, though, Mark opened up to me on the plane. I learned about his studies, and his girlfriend. I found out that he was an avid surfer, and that was one of the reasons why he was so excited to relocate to Southern California. The three of us talked all the way back to San Diego, and I found out more about my brother than I had ever known.

At some point, the conversation turned from what was going on in his life, presently, to what happened to everyone in the past. Specifically, Mark wanted me to know how everyone was feeling about me, in light of all that had gone down between me and the rest of the family over the years.

"Serena, I'm really glad that we have this time to talk," he said. "I kind of promised Luke that I would give you a chance and he was the one who suggested that I ride back with you. I'm all for that, especially since I really needed to get rid of my hoopdie anyhow." He smiled. "I'm going to miss that old girl, though. She and I have gone through a lot."

"Luke wanted you to reconnect, huh?"

"Yeah. Listen, I don't know if you know this. You probably do, but I'll tell you anyhow. Ever since you and Luke have been on better terms, he's been urging everyone else to do the same. That's why we all went out of our way to talk to you on this trip. I confess, I didn't want to come on this airplane trip with you. You've really been shitty to the family over the years. But I think that you're really trying to be a better person, and I know that you've gotten counseling. I see that you have changed, and, while I'm hesitant to trust you, I think that I'm willing to try."

"Thank you. That's all that I can ask. I might never fully get your love and respect, nor Amy's for that matter, but if you guys can just see past all that water under the bridge, I think that we can all be a family again."

Mark smiled and took another sip of his drink. He was drinking a Tanqueray and tonic, and Slade was sipping a neat scotch. I had elected to stay off the alcohol for this trip, just because I had drunk far too much over the course of the weekend, and I needed a break.

We made more small talk through the trip, and the plane finally touched down at Lindbergh Field around midnight. Slade had arranged for a limo to take Mark his house, and, before Mark got into the car, he embraced me. "It's really good to get to know you," he said. "I live in town, so don't be a stranger."

"I won't." I put my hand in his hair. "It's good to see you, too. Take care of yourself."

"I will."

And he was gone.

I watched him drive away and then I turned to Slade. "Well, we're back. I guess tomorrow I need to go ahead and move back to my place. That might appease Charlotte just a little, won't it?"

"I hate to say it, but I think that you're right about that." He took a deep breath. "I need to try to settle things again with Charlotte."

When he said that last part, I felt a well of panic start to rise up in my throat. Slade had hinted that he might have to give Charlotte what she wanted, in order to save me, and I hated to think about what that would mean. I knew what Charlotte wanted – she wanted to be Mrs. Slade Bridgewell. She had wanted that, apparently, since she was young. Would Slade be forced to do that? Would I allow that to happen?

I shook my head. No, I would never allow that to

happen. No matter what, I was going to fight for Slade until the bitter end. It might cost me my life, but, then again, I couldn't imagine life without Slade. I couldn't imagine what it would be like to see Slade and Charlotte in the society pages all the time. To see his pasted-on smile as he became a part of the Hollywood Elite, along with that awful witch. I knew that Charlotte wanted her and Slade to be some kind of power couple, the kind of couple who would be in the tabloids all the time and would generally rule the movie industry with an iron fist.

"Okay. Well, listen, I have to face the music with your mother. I know that. As much as I dread it, I have to get going on that case again. Tomorrow."

We headed to Slade's home, and, because both of us were dead tired, we hit the pillow and fell fast asleep.

The next day, I gave Margot a call. The call went to voice mail, so I left a message. "Margot, this is Serena. Give me a call back as soon as you can. We need to prepare you for some upcoming depositions, and we have to talk about what's going to happen next. Thanks."

Slade came in the room. "What's up?" he asked.

"Nothing. I just left a message for Margot to call me back. I called her earlier this morning as well. I'm really going to have to get rolling with this case if we're going to get everything done on time. I need to schedule depositions, and gather some more evidence, and I need her to be there every step of the way."

"Of course. Well, keep trying."

"Yes. Well, then, since I can't get a hold of her, let's just go on over to her house. She should be there, right?"

"Right. Why she's not picking up the phone, I have no clue. But she rarely leaves the house, so she should be around."

Slade and I spent the rest of the morning packing up our stuff. I was tired of going back and forth, and, truth be told, I really was looking forward to relaxing in my own home. As much as I loved to stay with Slade, and felt protected with him, I also felt that I needed my own space. I missed my routine of running on the beach and coming home to a glass of wine and a book. I knew that if Slade and I got married, though, it would be different, because I would feel that any house that we bought together would be ours. Right now, I was staying at Slade's, and I felt that way, too.

"Well, we need to go on over there," Slade said. "We need to get moving on her case. I hate to surprise her, but she really needs to pick up the phone when you call her." He looked annoyed and shook his head. "I hate it when people don't answer their phones, when you know that they're around."

Slade and I headed to Margot's house. It had been several hours since I first called her, and she still hadn't called back. While I wondered about that, I wasn't overly worried. I often didn't pick up the phone when people called me, simply because I didn't always feel like talking. That was probably the case with Margot, too.

We got to her house, which was in Solana Beach. It was a beautiful Tudor-style home with the traditional wood paneling on the front of the house and the traditional pitched roof. My favorite type of tree, a Date Palm, stood in the front yard. It was at least fifty feet tall, with a thick trunk and fronds that were thick and hanging down the side.

"Nothing. Listen, I'm not thinking really clearly, but I think that we're obviously going to have an autopsy." He looked down at the ground and pulled his hands through his hair again. "We have to find out what happened. But goddammit, what if they find something in her system? Some poison or something like that? What the hell would that prove?"

I knew where his mind was. It was on Charlotte, and the possibility that she was behind it. "Charlotte?"

"Damned straight." He sat down on one of the chairs and put his head in his hands. "Damned straight." Then he abruptly stood up again. "Fuck!" he shouted at the top of his lungs. "Fuck that fucking psychotic bitch."

"Slade, I…"

"She won't get you. I swear to god, she won't get you. She won't." He shook his head again, and started to pace the floor once more.

Just then, I saw the unmistakable flashing lights. It was the ambulance, and they were coming to take Margot to the hospital morgue. I looked out the window and saw two guys with a gurney preparing to mount the steps to Margot's home. When I saw that, I went downstairs to greet them.

"Upstairs," I said in a low voice as they came in the door.

"I'm very sorry for your loss," one of the guys said.

I said nothing, but just nodded my head.

They mounted the steps to the bedroom with me right behind them. Slade was sitting in the chair again, but he was perfectly still. He didn't even react to the men who were entering the room. He was just staring off into space, not saying a single word. One of the guys was trying to ask him questions, but he didn't respond.

I finally stepped in. "We came in the door and found

her lying there just like that. I don't think that there's a suicide note around, so we're not quite sure what happened. She was only 43 years old. She was sick with Hepatitis, but that was being treated and was under control."

One of the guys just nodded his head and started talking into the receiver on his shoulder. "Forty-three year old woman," he said. "Looks like the time of death was less than six hours ago." He was examining her. "No signs of trauma. She apparently was suffering from Hepatitis although that was under control."

"So, what's next?" I asked the man.

"We'll take her to the hospital morgue and if her next of kin would like to request an autopsy, then they're free to do so." He motioned to Slade, who was still sitting in the chair, apparently in shock.

"I think that will be necessary," I said. "When does Slade have to authorize that?"

"As soon as possible. It's not necessary to do it within 24 hours, although it's helpful to."

I went over to Slade and sat down next to him. "Slade," I said softly. "They're going to take Margot now. We should follow along behind them, don't you think? Then we can..."

Slade said nothing, but just nodded his head. "I know. I heard every word. I know."

"Okay. So, let's just get in the car and follow them over to the hospital."

He shook his head. "No. I can't do that right now. Maybe tomorrow, or the next day. But, right now, there's something that I have to do."

"Slade, don't do anything rash."

"I will. Goddammit, this ends tonight. Tonight. I don't care what I have to do, but it ends tonight. She won't cause any more problems. I won't let her."

"Slade, you have no proof that Charlotte is behind this."

"Oh, don't I? Don't I? I told you that I thought that she was on the edge of doing something and my hunch was right. I thought that she was going to attack you, and believe me, you're next. Goddammit. How do I have such a fucking psycho in my life? How?"

"Slade, your mother was sick and under a great deal of stress. She's lived a hard life. Maybe it all just caught up with her."

"Goddammit, Serena, how can you be so fucking naïve? You think that this is all a coincidence? We go away for the weekend, and I'm feeling uneasy about the psycho bitch, and we come back and my mother is dead. You think that I'm crazy for having this feeling that Charlotte is behind all of this? Tell me I'm crazy. Tell me."

I opened my mouth, but shut it again. I had to admit, Slade was making sense. Not that there was any solution to any of it. "Before you go and confront Charlotte, make sure that she did something. You don't want to go up there and piss her off if the autopsy comes back with natural causes."

He literally threw up his hands. "I don't care if I piss her off. Can't you see that? She's done so many psychotic things that have done nothing but ruin my life. And I can already see what's next. She'll be emboldened if she gets away with this. She'll be emboldened, and then suddenly, you'll meet your end on some road because you won't have brakes. Or there might be a car bomb. Those are just two of the ways that her family takes care of people who cross them."

"Well, then, perhaps what happened to your mother was just a coincidence. Her brakes weren't cut, and there wasn't a car bomb."

His eyes got wide, and, for just a second, I was a bit fearful. "You didn't just say that. You can't possibly have said that. As if the Garancinos just use two ways to kill people. I simply said that those are two of their main ways of taking care of their adversaries. I did not imply, in any way, shape or form, that those were the only means."

I was the lawyer, and I was going to have to come up with some better arguments if I was going to keep Slade from going to Charlotte's and raising hell. I didn't know why, but I had a strong feeling that if Slade actually confronted Charlotte, that there would be hell to pay. I knew, I just knew, that he would do more harm than good.

"Slade, look at me. Look at me, and listen to me. I don't want you to speak until I've said my piece."

Slade was up and pacing the floor again and I was having a hard time making eye contact with him. At some point, though, he did finally look at me. He stared at me with blank eyes, and then they came into focus. For a brief second, though, it looked like he wanted to kill somebody. Somebody like Charlotte.

"Okay," he finally said. "Say your piece."

I took a deep breath and patted the side of the couch. Slade stood there in front of me, and then reluctantly sat down next to me. "You can't go up to Charlotte's," I said. "Not now. You have no idea what happened to your mother, and, even if the autopsy comes back with some type of poison in her system, that still doesn't prove anything. You have to remember that Margot was possibly suicidal as it was."

"She wasn't suicidal. She was never suicidal. No matter what she went through in life, she always chose life. So you don't know what the fuck you're talking about."

His words stung, but I knew for a fact that he had been through some severe trauma, so I let it slide. "I might not know what I'm talking about, but I'm trying to slow you down here. The last thing that you want to do is make the whole situation worse."

"I'm not going to make the situation worse. I'm going to carefully plan what's going to happen before I get there."

"You might say that, but you were ready to go up there with guns blazing. That's the last thing that you need to do."

He shook his head and then put his head in his hands. "I can't lose you," he said softly. "But I have a feeling I'm going to. Something is going to happen to cause me to lose you. And it will be Charlotte's doing." He looked completely defeated and my heart went out to him. "Either you'll end up dead or I'll end up in prison for killing Charlotte. And killing her wouldn't do any good, either, because then her family will come after both you and me. I've been trying to figure out this whole thing eight ways to Sunday, and, so far, I've come up with nothing."

"Let's both try to figure this out," I said. "There has to be something that can be done to ensure everyone's safety."

"What? The blackmail thing was supposed to do the trick, but apparently it hasn't. Her agent can tell you that Charlotte is ready to jump, and is preparing for the media fallout that will inevitably occur when those documents about her past are made public. That means that she's about to become really dangerous."

"We don't know…"

"Serena, just stop. Stop. I'm in love with you. I can't tell you how much I think about you, every single minute of every single day. But Charlotte has put me into another impossible position. I just wish that you didn't find that goddamned video of Malcolm killing Jordan. I wish that I would have gone through with my original plan to take the fall for Jordan's murder, in exchange for your safety and that of my mother. There's not much that can be done now. The damage probably can't be contained."

"Slade, you can't do what you're going to do. I won't allow it." I was so afraid that Slade was going to end up giving Charlotte exactly what she wanted, and that would spell the end of his relationship with me.

"Tell me something better. Tell me something that will be fool-proof in ensuring your safety. Tell me that, and I'll take giving Charlotte what she wants off the table."

"I don't know of anything fool-proof exactly. Nothing ever is, and that's especially true in this case. But we could do something like speak to somebody who is high up in her family."

"And say what?"

"Tell them what's going on. Tell them that I'm a totally innocent party, and that I shouldn't be in their line of fire. Mafia people are reasonable sometimes, aren't they?"

Slade suddenly broke into a huge grin. I wasn't sure what to make of that, so I let him speak. "You really are that naïve, aren't you?" He shook his head. "I don't know how you, being from New York and being a criminal defense attorney, working with mobsters, can even talk like that at all. Unless you're not being serious."

I wasn't being all that serious, but I wanted to still throw it out there.

We sat next to one another on the couch for what seemed like hours. There was nothing left to say, really. I was trying to think of a solution to our problem with Charlotte, but nothing was coming to me. Nothing was apparently coming to Slade, either, because he just stopped speaking.

"Well," he finally said. "I'm a bit calmer now. I do want to go up and talk to Charlotte, but not until we get the results of the autopsy back. I suppose you're right – talking to her right now isn't going to do any good, and there are no good actions that I can take to make things go my way. Until I come up with a good plan, there's not much that can really be done."

"Okay," I said. I was feeling better about things, just because it seemed like I was buying some time with Slade. It might have been only a matter of days, or even hours, but buying time was the best that I could do at that point. "So, we need to go to the hospital, so that you can sign papers to authorize an autopsy. And then, I guess, I should also look for a new job."

"You can't do that yet. Not until I get a handle on what Charlotte is going to do. Things are right on the edge, and I don't want you to do anything that is going to push her over that edge."

"Slade, I'm going to be living next to Derek. I should think that I'll be sufficiently tormented."

"Think again." Then he shook his head. "Oh, what am I saying? I'm asking you to stay on a job that makes you uncomfortable, for good reason, just because I'm afraid of what the psycho is going to do. Goddammit, she shouldn't be dictating our lives like this."

"She shouldn't be, but she is. She is, and she will be, until we can figure out a plan to contain her. And, thus far, we haven't hit upon that plan."

"You're right." His shoulders were slumped, and he looked like he wanted to crawl right into the floor. "Well, we better go to the hospital. I'll authorize an autopsy, and then we'll have to figure something out. I won't leave you alone, though, with that Derek guy. I can understand that you want to return to your home, but I'd like to be there with you."

I suddenly felt shy. "You mean, you want to move in with me?"

When I asked that, he seemed to back away. "No. I mean, I want to stay with you as much as possible."

That confused me just a bit. Slade was always, in my view, trying to put just a little bit of distance between him and me. It was just a feeling that I got, that made me uncomfortable, but I felt unbalanced by him. "I'd like for you to stay with me as much as possible," I said. I wanted to go further and ask him why he didn't want to move in, but I stopped short. I didn't want to lay that on him when he was grieving for his mother.

"Well, let's go. I hope you don't mind driving. I don't feel up to driving just yet. I hope that you understand."

"Of course. You've been through some serious trauma. I wouldn't think to ask you to drive right now."

We stood up, and I took his hand. He gripped it tightly, and we made our way out to his car.

Then we took off. I didn't know what was going to happen in our near future, so I knew that we had to take everything one step at a time.

And the first step was going to be with Slade to do the last thing that I knew that he wanted to do - sign the autopsy authorization.

Chapter Twenty

We went to the hospital and Slade did what he needed to do. He signed the autopsy authorization and then we went back to my home. It was late by this time – the clock read just after midnight.

I felt awful for Slade. When I closed my eyes, I could feel the depth of his emotions. I could feel the grief, the sadness, and the rage, emanating from every one of his pores. I could feel his despair in my bones.

It was so sad. We had one of the greatest weekends of our lives, when we went to New York to see my brother get married. We went from something so pure, so filled with love, to dealing with the death of Slade's beloved mother, all in the span of a few days. What was ironic was that I was mending fences with my family, right when Slade was losing his.

As we drove to my home and the reality of what we had to face, Slade was silent. In his silence, I was able to feel his emotions even stronger. I didn't have his voice to distract me. I was starting to feel what he was feeling, without even trying to tune into it. His grief was that powerful.

"What's on your mind?" I finally asked him. I knew the answer to that question, but I wanted to get him talking if he wanted to.

He shook his head. "She was my only family." He paused for a few seconds. "That's not fair. Scott was a good adoptive father. But she was my only real family. She had such a hard time in life, and it just seems so unfair. That's all."

"I know how you feel," I said. "When my mother was killed, it was like a part of me was violently ripped out. I felt this hole right in the center of my soul." I put my hand on his. "Sudden deaths are the worst, because it's such a shock. Such a huge, huge shock. And when a young person gets cut down, it makes it that much worse. My mother, and yours, should have lived to be old and grey. But they didn't. They didn't, and it doesn't seem fair or right."

Slade just stared out the window and didn't say anything. I felt uncomfortable, wanting to fill the silence, but knowing that filling the silence wasn't what was called for here. I had to follow Slade's cues, and, thus far, the only cue he was giving me was that he wasn't in the mood to talk.

I took a deep breath, and talked quietly to myself. "Don't push, don't push, don't push," I said to myself. I looked over at Slade, who hadn't moved since he got into the car. However, his facial expression was different. He no longer looked blank, but looked pissed. Then he looked blank again. I knew what was going on – he was trying not to think, but, every so once in awhile, he would think about Charlotte and would get angry. I couldn't read his mind, but I knew him, and I knew that this was what was going on. I didn't know what to say to him, but I knew what was on his mind.

He surprised me, though, when about a half hour after we got on the road, he addressed my earlier comment about my mother. "I know you can relate, Serena. I can't even imagine how much pain you felt when your mother was taken from you like that." And that was all he said. After he said that, he looked out the window again.

We drove along like that until we got to my home. We ended up at my house around three in the morning and I headed straight into my bedroom and lay down. Slade was soon lying beside me, and he just wrapped his body around me. He held me tight, so tight that I felt that I couldn't breathe. Yet, I lay perfectly still and let him hold me like that. He was asking for comfort without actually asking for it, and that was what I was going to give him.

For the rest of the night, he held me like he was using me as a lifeline.

I had never felt closer to him.

Chapter Twenty-One

I had to go to work the next day. Actually, it wasn't the next day so much as it was later on in the morning. We had gotten in at around 3, and I woke up again around 7, with the intention of getting into the office by 8. I didn't really want to leave Slade, of course, but he assured me that he was okay. "Go into work," he said. "I think that I need to be alone anyhow."

"If you're sure…"

"Of course. Listen, I know that you have cases piled up, and I would imagine that your firm will give you even more to do, now that you don't have my mom's case anymore. I'm fine, and I'll see you this evening when you get off."

"What are you going to do today?"

"I think that I'll go ahead and schedule a Skype meeting. I need to start making plans to get back into it full-time, now that I don't have a reason to stay away."

I bit my lip when he said that. He still hadn't addressed with me what he wanted me to do once he returned to his firm in LA. Now he was saying that he didn't have a reason to stay away. I wanted to scream "what about me? Aren't I a good enough reason to stay away?" But I didn't. He was dealing with overwhelming grief, and I didn't want to add to that.

I went over to kiss him goodbye, and we embraced before I left.

When I got into work, I immediately went to my office and shut the door. I had no desire to make conversation with anyone there, and I really just wanted to hunker down and shut out the rest of the world. I especially didn't want to see Derek.

Unfortunately, Derek wanted to see me.

He came into my office about a half hour after I went in there with the door locked. I had no idea how he managed to unlock the door. "Serena, where have you been?" he asked me. "I know that your boyfriend owns this firm, but that doesn't mean that you can just make your own hours."

I took a deep breath. Derek had been laying low for several weeks, and now, here he was, trying to intimidate me once again. "None of your fucking business," I said. "I have a lot of work to do, since I've been gone for so long, so if you'll excuse me." I started to write down notes about a case and picked up the phone to call my assistant, Anita. I needed to get some discovery requests out the door, along with some interviews set up with some key figures in an embezzling case that had landed on my desk while I was gone.

Derek got closer to me, and I tried to calm my racing heart. "The door's locked," he said, coming around behind me.

Alarm bells were going off inside my head when he walked behind me. I had no idea what he was going to do.

To my horror, he put a ball gag around my head, like

Slade would do to me when we were playing. I couldn't make a sound. "You like this, don't you, Serena?" he whispered to me. "I know you do. You get off on this kind of thing. Being controlled, being helpless. I know it. I knew it then. I gave you just what you wanted that night, and, ever since then, I've been thinking about the moment when I would give it to you again."

I had no idea what to do. I stood up abruptly, and prepared to run screaming from the room, but the second I stood up, he pushed me back down. "Where are you going?" he asked me.

Then he spun me around, and I was face to face with his cruel expression. Gone was any hint of civility on his face. What I was looking at was a pair of dead blue eyes. His mouth was contorted, as if he were in pain. "Nobody will hear you scream, Serena. I guess because you cannot scream." He brought out a knife, and he put it to my throat. "Charlotte has asked me to do this, but, I have to say, I was quite happy when she told me what I was supposed to do. I remember your tight pussy. It was tight that night because I was your first. I doubt it's still that tight, but no matter. I'm quite sure that it still feels nice."

He was leaning down, both his hands on the sides of my chair. I was looking up, facing him with the ball gag in my mouth.

"Why did Charlotte want me to do this?" he asked me. "I know that's what you're thinking right now. I'll tell you why. She wants you to be traumatized. So traumatized that you push Slade away. That's why. She also just wants you to suffer. She's kind of a bitch, that one, but she pays me very well." He got closer to me, his lips just centimeters from mine. "She pays me well, but I really should be paying her. It would be worth it to me, because getting in your pussy again has been something that I've been thinking about for many years."

He spread my legs, and I started to panic. My first inclination would be to punch him again, but the last thing that I wanted to do was to land a punch that would only serve to piss him off. The punch at the restaurant was effective, because I was around a lot of people, and Derek wouldn't have done anything. But here…we were alone, the door was locked, and I couldn't speak or scream.

When he unzipped his pants and exposed himself and then yanked down my panties while he hiked up my skirt, the panic that began when he gagged me came to a crescendo. He was going to do this to me again, and I was determined not to let him. I wanted to kick him right in the nuts, which were exposed, so I knew that I would drop him to his knees. But I couldn't. He had both of my ankles held firmly in his hands, and, when I tried to move them, I couldn't. He was way too strong.

I was going to have to use my fists again. He had both of my ankles held, which meant that he wasn't going to be able to fend off my fists. He leaned down, his hard cock reaching my opening. His face was within centimeters of mine again, and I poked him, hard, in his right eye.

That seemed to do the trick. He reflexively lowered his head and, just as reflexively, both of his hands went to his injured eye. That meant that my legs were free, so I kicked him, hard, right in his exposed nuts. He crumpled to the ground, and I hurriedly got up from my chair, and ran out the door. He was on his feet and chasing me, but I managed to get out the door before he was able to slam it.

My heart pounding, I ran to the front door of the office suite, after hastily taking off the ball gag. "I'm leaving for the day," I told the receptionist. "Hold all my calls."

"Will do," she said. "When will you be back?"

Never. "I don't know right now. I just know that I have to leave. I'm not feeling well."

She looked skeptical. "Okay. But, listen, I know that it's not my business, but everyone's been noticing how much time you've been away. We all know that your boyfriend owns this firm. I don't want you to get into trouble, but everyone is starting to talk." She nodded her head knowingly. "I only wanted to tell you that, because I've been where you are, and it's not fun."

"Good," I said. "All the more reason for me to leave this place." When I said those words, I realized that I wouldn't be back. Ever. I also realized that I was going to have to move out of my house. There was no way that I was going to live next to that man. I somehow thought that he wasn't going to try something, but, now that I knew what his intentions were, there wasn't any way that I could ever be around him.

Fuck Charlotte. I knew that getting away from Derek was going to set her off, but I didn't care. I would sooner die than be raped again.

"Okay," she said. "But don't ever say that I didn't warn you."

"I consider myself warned."

At that, I left.

I left, and there wasn't any way that I would be coming back.

Leaving might cost me my life, but so be it. I couldn't live like this.

Chapter Twenty-Two

The first thing that I did when I left the office was go to the beach. I needed to feel calm, and the water always did that for me. When I got there, it was noon, and the beach was crowded but not as crowded as it was during the summertime. There were people everywhere, even in the water, and I shivered just a little. It was October and Indian Summer had evidently passed, because there was just the slightest chill in the air. Not that it was cool, because it wasn't by any means.

I took off my shoes and stood in the water, which lapped at my calves and knees. Every once in awhile, a big wave would come in, but I didn't care. I was stilled dressed in my business suit, and I was getting soaked, but I let the waves come in and envelope me.

A few minutes later, I was coming down just a little bit from the fear and helplessness I had felt in that office and the tears started to come. They mingled with the water on my face, and I sat down in the sand. Again, I wasn't even thinking about the fact that I was ruining my nice clothes.

All I could think of was how good it felt for the water to spray on my face and surround me.

I became aware that there was a small child who was watching me with wonder. She was about two years old with blonde curly hair. She had a shovel in one of her hands and her other hand was in her mouth and she just stared at me. Then she sat down too and dropped the shovel and put that chubby little hand on my arm. For some reason, that kind gesture from the tiny child just made me cry even more. I brought my knees up and I put my head down and just bawled. The child was sitting next to me for several minutes, her little hand petting my arm and shoulder.

The child's mother finally noticed what was happening and she came up and snatched her arm. The little girl protested and continued to try to hold onto me while she started crying as well. "You have to come with me, Miranda," the mother said. "That water will come and sweep you away."

"No," she said defiantly.

The mother seemed exasperated by the tone of her voice. Then, she too, put her arm around me. "Miss, are you okay?" Her voice was now gentle and soothing.

I seemed to snap back into reality with the mother's voice, and I finally realized how I probably looked. I just nodded my head, but she didn't seem convinced. "Miss, please stand up. I don't want to call the lifeguard."

I reluctantly got to my feet and looked at the slight woman. She was dressed in a tankini that showed off her buff arms and abs. With her blonde hair and deep tan, she looked like a typical Southern California beach girl. "Thanks," I said.

"Not a problem," she said, putting her arm around me.

"Come with me," she said, pointing to the rows of homes that faced the beach. "I live right over here."

I felt like a zombie as she led me to her home. It was a three-story place that had high ceilings and an open floor plan. She sat me down on her couch after putting down a towel. "Is there anybody you would like for me to call?"

I shook my head.

"My name is Rebekah by the way."

"Serena."

I soon had a cup of tea in front of me and a blanket over my shoulder. "Serena, I'd like to look at your phone." She gestured to my small bag which was what I had carried with me on my person when I was in the water. "Is it in there?"

I had no idea why she wanted my phone, but I nodded my head.

She took it out of the bag. "Do you mind if I look through your missed calls?"

My mind was fuzzy and again, I had no clue on why she was asking these questions. I simply couldn't process it. I just nodded my head again, and she looked through the calls.

"Slade," she said. "Is that your husband?"

I shook my head.

"Boyfriend?"

I nodded my head.

"Do you mind if I call him?"

I shook my head.

At that, she got on the phone. "Hello, my name is Rebekah. May I please speak with Slade?"

After a brief pause, she said, "Serena is here with me. I hate to bother you, but could you please come to my house at your earliest convenience? I live on Mission Beach." She paused again. "It's the first house you get to after you pass by the bars and other businesses." She nodded her head. "I'll see you in a few. Thank you."

"Your boyfriend will be here in a few minutes. He sounds like a great guy – he didn't ask any questions, he just said that he would be here and he was leaving his house right now.

"He lives in Del Mar," I said weakly. "So it'll be awhile."

I sipped my tea and Rebekah took a seat in a big chair next to the couch I was sitting on. She obviously had no idea what to say to me, because she sat there silently. The little girl, whose name was apparently Miranda, came up to me again and she, too, watched me silently.

"Is there anything I can do for you?" Rebekah asked me.

I had to make my mind a blank, because if I didn't, I felt that I would lose it. What happened to me in that office was bringing back the horrible memories of what had happened to me back in the woods all those years ago. I didn't want to examine what was roiling underneath my psyche. There was the possibility that I would have a mental breakdown from all the stress, combined with the terror that almost befell me with Derek.

"No," I said, suddenly feeling that I couldn't wait to see Slade. "But thank you. Thank you for your kindness."

"There's no need to thank me." She smiled. "It's my daughter who found you and paid attention to what was happening. Children can be so perceptive sometimes. You know?"

I managed a weak smile. "I'll be okay. I just had something happen to me and it's bringing up stuff that I hadn't really wanted to face for a long time." Rebekah was a perfect stranger, yet I found myself wanting to tell her everything. She just had that kind of face and demeanor. "But I'll get through this."

"Do you want to talk about it?"

I nodded my head. "Yes. There's this man who is tormenting me and he almost did something to me in my office. It's the same man who actually did something to me when I was only 18. And I guess I just had some kind of a flashback."

I suddenly knew just how Margot had felt when Hugh was standing in her living room. PTSD was like that – an experience can trigger you and, suddenly, you're right back where you were when you first had the trauma. I knew that was what was happening to me.

She poured me another cup of tea. "I wish I had words to help you." She glanced at the clock. "Hopefully your boyfriend will be here soon."

And, as if on cue, there was a ringing of the doorbell.

Rebekah opened the door, and Slade walked in. He saw me and immediately went over to me. "Serena, what's going on?" he asked me as he kneeled right in front of me. He put his hand on my leg. "What's going on?"

I opened my mouth, but nothing came out.

"She's had some sort of encounter with a man that has her scared," Rebekah said.

All at once, Slade's face changed. He looked like a man possessed.

"Mom's tests came back," he said quietly. "They found traces of poison in her system." He shook his head. "This has to end."

"Slade, what are you going to do?" I asked him desperately.

"I'm going to do what I have to. I have to make sure that you're safe from now on. You don't have to tell me what happened – it's written all over your face. She got to my mother, and she's getting to you by using that bastard Derek. I'll deal with him later, too, but I have to get to the root of the problem. I need to cut the head off of the problem the best way that I can."

He put his arms around me and held me close. "You're going to be safe, Serena. You will be. I'll make sure of that."

I couldn't help myself – I just let loose a torrent of tears. "I can handle this, Slade. I've already decided that I'm going to quit my job and I'm going to move away from that house. I thought that I could face this head-on, but I don't think that I can. But I'll handle it in my own way."

"No. That's not good enough."

Slade stood up, and he picked me up in his arms. I wrapped my arms around his neck, and he held out a hand to shake Rebekah's hand. "I can't thank you enough. I'm sorry, I didn't get your name."

Rebekah shook his hand. "Rebekah, and don't mention it. I was on the beach, and I saw her sitting in the surf, fully clothed. My little daughter went over to her, and I knew that she needed help. Anybody would have done the same."

"Well, thank you," he said. "I have to get Serena home, but I want you to know that meeting you gives me some kind of faith that there are good people out in the world."

Rebekah nodded her head. "Lots of good people in the world. But thank you for saying that."

At that, Slade carried me to his car, which was parked on the street next to Rebekah's house. He gently strapped me in. "This is neither here nor there, but I'm going to send her a nice thank-you gift," he said. "Now, tell me what happened."

"Derek attacked me," I said.

Slade gripped the steering wheel and stared straight

ahead. His jaw was clenched, and his hands were gripping the steering wheel so tightly I thought that his knuckles were going to turn white. "Attacked you," he said slowly. "Meaning?"

"Not raped me, but he came close." I was able to tell him the story because just being around him calmed me down considerably. "He came into my office, even though the door was locked, and I told him to leave. He didn't, but came around behind me and put a gag on my mouth. And then he controlled my legs and…"

Slade was breathing in and out slowly. "And?"

"Well, he took off my underwear and he took down his pants. Before he could do anything else, I poked him in his eye and then kicked him right in the nuts." It was then that I started to laugh hysterically. "Oh boy, you should have seen the look on his face when I did that. I kicked him right in his bare nuts with my high heels. I'd be surprised if he's not in the hospital." I shook my head. "Bastard." And then I continued to laugh hysterically until tears were streaming down my cheeks.

Slade wasn't laughing with me, of course. He was staring straight ahead at the road. "I'm going to kill him," he said quietly. "I will kill him."

"Slade, don't be dumb. If you kill him, then you'll definitely be in prison and there really won't be any way out this time." I was thinking clearly for the first time in hours, and I attributed that 100% to Slade. "Trust me, I've had plenty of clients who've killed to protect their woman's honor, and they're the ones who end up raped in prison for the rest of their lives."

"I don't give a shit. He can't do that and get away with it." Then he shook his head. "No. I'll kick his ass again, but the person I really want to kill is the one who put him up to all of this. Her ass is the one that I really want to kick. Derek is just a sick pawn. He's nobody and he's nothing to her, and she's probably going to destroy him once he's of no use to her."

"Again, Slade, you can't do anything to her. If you do, her family will have you killed so fast…"

"And what? What? If I don't deal with her, she'll get you. She's getting bold, and I need to know exactly why and exactly what her next moves are. She's sending these messages to us – these messages are telling me that she's about to escalate. You won't be safe if she does that."

"We'll run. You have a home in Italy, and we can live there."

"Italy? Italy?" He snorted. "Good thinking there, Serena, going to the old country. If you think that the Garancinos are powerful here, then you haven't seen how powerful they are in Italy. That's probably one of the dumbest ideas I've ever heard."

All at once, I was angry at Slade. "So, what's your plan? What is it? I'm throwing stuff out there, but I don't hear any good ideas coming out of your mouth."

I didn't notice it, but we had arrived at my home. "I'm going to buy some time," he said.

I didn't like the sound of that.

I knew what "buying time" was going to entail, and I didn't like that idea one bit.

Chapter Twenty-Three

We got into my front door, and I immediately realized that the dogs weren't in the house. In my panic, I completely forgot to pick them up from the day care center.

"Don't worry," Slade said. "I called the place and they're fine."

"Thanks."

"Serena, I don't want you to worry. Believe it or not, I do have a plan. I didn't want to tell you about it, because it's something that you won't like at all. But I've been thinking about this since I spoke with Charlotte's agent and realized that she's about to go outer limits. She's stepped everything up, assuming that she's behind my mother's..." He shook his head. "I still can't accept that she's gone."

"Slade, if the plan involves what I think that it involves, then I'm not on board with it."

"Of course you're not. But, at this point, there's only one way that I can think of to buy some time."

I wanted to slap him. Maybe a slap would knock some sense into his gorgeous head. "Slade, I..."

"Stop," he said, putting his hand on my mouth. "Tonight, it's you and me. Tomorrow is going to be a different story, but tonight, we have to enjoy each other's company."

I didn't like the sound of that, yet, when Slade put his hand in my hair, I somehow forgot all about the stress that had happened that day. He had a way of making me forget my own name sometimes.

Then he kissed me.

And then, as usual, I lost my breath.

Chapter Twenty-Four

I left Serena, and I headed to see Charlotte. I hated that I had been put in that situation, but I couldn't figure anything else out. Blackmailing her didn't work. Threatening her wasn't working. I could literally kill her, but Serena was right – that would cause more problems and it would be way too risky.

The only thing that I could possibly think of doing, right at that moment, was to play her game the way that she wanted me to play it. It turned my stomach and made me absolutely sick, but I was going to have to agree to marry her. That would buy me some time, and then I could possibly work a plan that would get her gone, once and for all.

Marrying her would afford me access to the inner-workings of her family, and it would give me some kind of road-map for how to deal with her. I'd be able to get to know her family, and I would be able to really find out who had what role in the Garancino organization, and it would give me an opportunity to try to work my way around all of them.

That was my plan. I had no clue if it was going to work, but it was all that I had right at that moment. Serena was against it, of course, but she hadn't offered me any other alternative. If she did, then maybe I would be able to avoid it.

Whatever happened, though, Serena would be safe. That was literally the only thing that mattered to me. I knew Charlotte, and I knew that she was days away from making her move. My mother was the opening shot. Derek's move showed that she was emboldened. It was only a matter of time before I found Serena dead, and then I, too, would be dead. Maybe not literally dead, but dead inside. Serena was the love of my life, and I needed to protect her at all costs.

As I drove up to Los Angeles, it felt like the drive was the longest of my life. I was determined to follow through, but that determination, combined with the thought that I was doing the only thing possible to ensure Serena's safety, didn't make any of it any easier.

I got to her place, and the gate opened up. I drove up the long drive and rang the doorbell. She answered the door in a tight sweater that plunged and showed her cleavage. "Come on in," she said. I had called her before-hand, so she was expecting me. "Let's talk out on the balcony."

I wanted to strangle her, and it took every ounce of will-power to prevent me from doing so. I followed her out to the balcony, where she had set the table outside with candles and a bottle of wine. It made me sick to think that she was already declaring victory, and this was her way of rubbing it in my face.

We sat down, and I refused a glass of wine. "Listen, Charlotte, I'm not going to beat around the fucking bush here. I have no idea what you're up to, but I'm literally hours away from blasting you to the media. You're going to be ruined, absolutely ruined, when I get through with you."

To my chagrin, she smiled. "No, actually, you won't be. It took me months, but I managed it."

I narrowed my eyes. "Managed what?"

"I've managed to destroy every single record that showed what I did in my past. That includes the record that you have on your computer. And the record on Serena's computer, and that douche-bag Lars' computer as well."

Crap. I had a feeling that what she did was something like this, but I couldn't be sure. "Bullshit. There's no way you could breach my security protocols to do something like that. I've had no evidence of a security breach. You're fucking bluffing."

Charlotte started to laugh. "You think that you're the only one with an Ace computer hacker? I have my own Lars, and he's good. He's so good that he was able to breach the security of your system without you even knowing it. Don't worry, he didn't commit espionage, although he could do that, too. He was only concerned with destroying those records. And the original doctor, the one who treated me? I took care of him, too, and his records." She smiled. "As I said, it wasn't easy at all, but I managed it. I mean, my computer guy managed it. You no longer have proof of anything at all."

"Bullshit," I said. I had copies of her records in about 20 different places on my computer, and I knew that this hacker guy, whoever he was, couldn't possibly get all of them without my knowledge.

"Check mate," she said gleefully. "Now, since you have nothing on me, I'm going to continue my reign of terror until I get what I want from you."

"I said bullshit."

"Bullshit what?" She shrugged her shoulders. "Maybe you still have some copies of those records, somewhere deep in the recesses of your system, but I no longer care about that. Because I have a backup plan. I'm not stupid."

"What's your backup plan?"

"It involves discrediting you, which will be so easy to do, considering how much trouble you've been in lately. First you murdered Jordan. I mean, you didn't really do that, but you'd be surprised about how many people think that you're still under suspicion and that you really did murder him." She raised her eyebrows. "Again, it took me months, but I've done focus group after focus group, and at least half the idiots in this country think that you did it, even though there's definitive evidence that you didn't. So, there's that."

I knew where this was going, and I had to admit, this psychotic bitch was brilliant. She was going to play the PR game, and she evidently got her ducks in a row.

She went on. "Oh, and you did dispose of a body. Everyone knows that, and you're good for that one. So, in society at large, you're still seen as a criminal, a violent one at that, and I'm...well, I'm America's new sweetheart. Once my publicity machine gets going, you're not going to be able to win."

"I've got a PR team that would beat the ass out of yours."

She rolled her eyes. "You're starting at a disadvantage, Slade. I know that your PR team is the best in the business, but so is mine. All things being equal, though, I have the leg-up on you, because half the country still thinks that you bludgeoned a man to death in cold blood."

I drew a breath, trying to calm down and not lunge at this woman and strangle her. *I didn't kill Jordan, but I will kill you, bitch.*

She just smiled. "So, I get the PR machine going, and the story is going to be that you forged those records. And who's going to contradict you? I took care of the Doctor who treated me, and trust me, after my family got through with him, nobody else is ever going to talk to media to corroborate your story."

"I don't believe you." I hadn't heard that her treating doctor was killed, so I figured this was another one of her bluffs.

She calmly showed me her computer, and I almost vomited when I saw the news story that she was showing me. The doctor who diagnosed her, Dr. Valenti, was found burned to death in the trunk of a car. "This was just a warning to anybody who wants to talk to the media and tell them what happened with me and that unfortunate incident in my past and my unfortunate diagnosis. Trust me, everyone has gotten that message. Nobody will ever talk to the media."

I leaned back. It was just as I had suspected – Charlotte had a plan to release her from my blackmailing her.

I thought that there was a glimmer of hope that I could somehow outfox her, but, right at that moment, I couldn't. I was going to have to put my own plan into action, and it was not only dangerous, but it was also heartbreaking.

Serena was going to be safe, though. That was all that mattered.

"You got me." I crossed my arms. "Let's do it. Let's get married."

She smiled. "I knew you would come around."

Wicked Temptations: Chapter One

Serena

Slade was due to come and talk to me, and I had to admit, I was nervous. Very nervous. He had hinted that he was going to have to do something drastic to make sure that I was safe, and I had a sneaking suspicion on exactly what that thing was going to be. No matter how many times I told him not to do anything that would jeopardize my relationship with him, I knew that he was going to go ahead with his plans. It wasn't going to be pretty.

As I saw him come up the driveway to my house, his head was hung, and I just knew. He didn't even have to tell me what was going on. It was written all over his gorgeous face.

I opened the door, and, without a word, I walked into the sun room. I patted my legs, and the dogs got up on the easy chair with me. Slade, also wordless, followed me into the room and sat across from me. He drew a breath and clenched his hands in front of him. He simply stared at me for the longest time, his beautiful eyes pained and haunted.

I stared back, not saying a single word. In my mind, I was thinking that, if neither of us spoke, maybe none of this would be true. There wouldn't be some kind of awful revelation that hung in the air, threatening to end us. I wouldn't be hearing from him about how he has no choice to marry that bitch, and how he was going to find a way out of it for both of us. How it would only be temporary, and that, soon enough, he and I would be together and there would no longer be a threat to my life. None of that would be true, if only neither of us spoke.

So, for what seemed like an eternity, I sat there, the dogs on my lap, and stared wordlessly at him and he did the same. His hands were still clenched in front of him, and, from time to time, he would hang his head and put his hands behind his neck. Then, a few minutes later, he would look up at me again with pain in his eyes.

Finally, he opened his mouth, as if to speak. At that point, I stood up.

"Don't say it, just don't say it. I already know what's going on. I already know what you told that bitch. And there's only one thing that I can say to you – get the fuck out of my house. Get the fuck out and never, ever come back."

He stood up as well, and attempted to put his arms around me. I pushed him away, violently. "Perhaps you didn't hear me. I want you to leave, and I want you to leave this very second. There is nothing that you can say to me that will make this right." I was being irrational, and a part of me knew it. A part of me, deep down in my soul, knew that what Slade was doing was not only the right thing, it was the only thing that could keep me alive. A part of me knew that what he was doing was sacrificing his own happiness so that I could be safe. That part of me loved him desperately.

The other part of me also loved him desperately, but hated him just as much. That part of me only wanted him and I to be together, no matter how that could be accomplished. That part of me literally didn't care if I lived or died, as long as I could be with him for the short time that I would be on this earth. And he couldn't see that. I hated that he couldn't see that.

These two distinct sides of me were at war as I looked at his beautiful eyes and face. He made no effort to leave, and that made me love, and hate, him all the more. "Serena," he finally said. "I know that you know what happened between Charlotte and me. I know that you know in your heart that I would never do anything like this unless it was absolutely necessary. I think that you also know that I'm going to be get a plan together that will make sure that you and I end up together for the rest of our lives without having a shadow hanging over us. I don't really know exactly what that plan is, but I'm buying time for us. I don't expect you to understand right now, but I would love it if you would please see this as buying our long-term future in exchange for some short-term misery."

I drew a breath. "When is the wedding?" I asked him. I didn't really want to know the answer to that question, of course. I only wanted him to know that I knew what was going on. I wanted to stick the knife into him and make him feel the pain that I felt. By forcing him to answer that simple question, I knew that he was going to feel what he was about to do. To him, to us, to our future. I wasn't buying the whole *I'm doing this now to make sure our future is secure* bullshit.

He could kiss my ass if he thought that I was buying that crap.

He sat back down and hung his head again, putting his hands behind his neck. "I don't know," he said quietly. "Soon. I need to get this over with so that I can start snooping around her family. I need to find a weak spot. I need to find a rat, somebody who is willing to double-cross her and perhaps, maybe, keep her in line." His eyes looked at me, sorrow filling them. "It's the only thing that I can think of right now."

I nodded my head. "Get out. Get out, and go marry your whore. Go marry her, and make sure that your face is in the tabloids at all times." I smiled. "And, trust me, you will be in the tabloids at all times. It's so fucking priceless, this story – rising Hollywood star marries handsome billionaire who was in the news for a murder he didn't commit. Who is currently about to stand trial for disposing a body and covering up a murder 20 years ago. The tabs are going to be all over that shit."

He crinkled up his brows. "Is that all that you're worried about? That you're going to be forced to see me every time you go to the grocery store?" He made a move, once again, to hold me in his arms, as he stood up and came over to me.

I backed away. With every step he took towards me, I took one step back. He wasn't going to act like nothing was wrong. He wasn't going to be able to just put his strong arms around me, and kiss me and make love to me, as if he wasn't going to be married to somebody else. I wouldn't let him do that. He couldn't get away with that, because I wasn't going to allow that. "Get away, Slade. I told you a few minutes ago that I wanted you gone, and I mean that. Stop the bullshit. You're going to marry that whore, and nothing will be done to save me or to save us. You're going to fall into that lifestyle, and you're going to forget that I exist. I already see that. So get out. Get out now."

"Serena," he began, as he once again wrapped his arms around me.

"No. You and I are done." I pushed him, hard, so hard that he fell on the floor. He apparently wasn't bracing himself. I closed my eyes, and left the room, with him still on the floor.

It didn't take him long, though, to get up off the floor and follow me into the living room.

"Slade, why are you still here? Get out. I told you to get out, and I mean it." I didn't mean it, of course. I desperately wanted him to stay there with me. I desperately *needed* him to stay there with me. But not like this. Not when I knew, *I knew*, that, the second he left the house, he would be leaving for good. He would leave this house and go to her, and, the next thing I would hear, would be news of his happy wedding with the Hollywood goddess. I wouldn't be able to turn on the television without seeing the two of them together. I had always loved to watch the Academy Awards on TV – that was one of my guilty pleasures, even if I hardly ever got to see the nominated movies – but I could never again watch that show, because *she* would be on there with *him*. I would want to vomit when I saw her smiling face, and he would also be smiling, because she would be telling him, behind the scenes, that he better smile *or else.*

Worse than that, though, would be the fact that Slade would no longer be in my life. My life was going to be as empty as it was before I met him, and I just couldn't handle that fact.

"Serena," he said. "I'm not going to even try to bullshit you. I respect and love you too much to do that. So, yes, after I leave, I'll be going to Charlotte's and I'm going to do the unspeakable. I know that there's nothing that I can say to you that will make you believe that this is best for us. I know that you'll never really believe that I'm going to find a way out of this and I'm going to return to you and make you my wife for real. You're going to hate me, and I don't blame you for hating me. I just have to get through these next few months, which are going to be absolute torture, so that I can fix this problem for good. You don't believe that though, and I don't blame you. But I love you, Serena, and, mark my words, we will be together after this. Together for real."

I drew a breath when he said the words *I'm going to make you my wife for real.* That was the first time that Slade had ever said something like that. I had always assumed that Slade wasn't serious about me and my long-term future with him, but, with those words, I knew that he was. That thought comforted me, even though the reality of the situation was that Slade and I, in all likelihood, would never see each other again after today.

I blinked back tears. This was such an impossible situation. The part of me that was desperately in love with him resurfaced for a moment, and I allowed him to come and put his arms around me. I felt his breath inhaling my scent, as if he never wanted to forget it. His masterful hands were gliding up and down the small of my back, and, as I laid my head on his chest, I heard his heart start to pound. I closed my eyes, wanting to stay there forever. If I was ever given a choice just to stand there with Slade, motionless, his arms around me, his heart pounding in my ears, forever, I would have taken it. Forget work, forget Charlotte, forget the world around us. I wanted just to stay there, exactly as we were, for the rest of time.

After what seemed like forever, Slade gently brought my face to his, and kissed me. His hands were on my cheeks, and I felt myself melt into him. Even though my mind was telling me not to do this – it was wrong, he was going to be gone soon, and making love with him would simply make me miss him that much more – my body was betraying me. I felt the heat in his kiss, and I could feel the urgency in it. Both of us knew the score. At least our minds did. But I knew that his body, and his soul, were feeling the need for the two of us to connect one last time. I was feeling the same.

I felt like I had no bones, and Slade picked me up and carried me to my bedroom. He laid me down on the bed, and, without a single word, he gently stripped me of my clothes. When his tongue met my clit, it wasn't with the urgency that he displayed in his earlier kiss, but, rather, it was slow and gentle. It was as if he had to make this last, and he knew it. Every stroke of his tongue brought me to new heights, because I had never felt so much connected to him. I had never before felt like this. It was as if he and I literally were one body, one mind, one heart, one soul. He became a part of me in that moment, and, when I orgasmed for that first time, it was as if it was my very first orgasm ever.

His hands and fingers made their way up my stomach and to my breasts, and his gentle tongue traced a trail up my breasts and to my neck. There was heat in his lips and tongue, heat that I never really felt before. His warmth was something that I had always noted about him, but it was something that I could feel at that moment, more than I had ever felt it in my life.

As I felt his rock-hard cock gently fill me up, I rocked into him, throwing my legs around his back.. I felt as if I never wanted to let him go. I wanted to imagine that I was holding him to me, and that I would hold him to me for the rest of both of our lives. In my head, that was exactly what was going to happen with us – I would keep him there with me, and he would never, ever leave.

He made love to me for the better part of an hour – so slow and gentle that it was almost agonizing. My clit was on fire with every gentle stroke of his glorious penis, which slowly but surely rocked in and out of me. I felt one orgasm after another roil through me. Our bodies were one. I couldn't tell where he ended and I began, or where I ended and he began.

When he finally, and reluctantly, withdrew from me, after I felt his hot cum roiling inside of me, he just looked at me. I looked back at him, and I nodded. There was nothing to say that hadn't already been said. Nothing to do that hadn't already been done.

It was finished. We both knew it. Whether it was finished forever, or just finished for a few months, was unknown. That remained to be seen.

In my mind, though, it was finished for good. I had to just forget about him. If I let myself pine away after him, then I could never move on with my life. And I had to do just that – move on with my life. From that point on, I would pretend like Slade didn't exist. I would just have to compartmentalize him like I always was able to before whenever tragedy struck me.

And that was what this was – a tragedy. Losing Slade was a tragedy.

Just like I moved past all my other tragedies, I would move past this one as well. In time.

At least I hoped that I would.

Wicked Temptations: Chapter Two

Slade

I left Serena, and I felt the weight of what had happened come down on me. Goddamn Charlotte. Goddamn her. She was ruining my life, and I knew that I was going to have to find a way out and soon. Very soon. If I had to kill her myself, I would do that. Of course, I didn't want to do that, but that was an option to me right at that moment. I had to admit, covering up that murder for my mother all those years ago gave me a certain kind of confidence that I could do it again. After all, that murder would have been unsolved if it weren't for Charlotte and her big, blackmailing mouth.

As I drove up the highway, my mind was filled with revenge. Revenge was the first thing on my mind, but somewhere, in the recesses of my brain, a plan was starting to formulate. It was hazy though, nascent. At some point, it was going to be fully formed, though, I knew. And then it was going to be put into action.

At that moment, though, I was going to have to face up

to what I had done and what was about to happen. As much as it made me want to vomit, I had to face it. I was desperately worried about Serena, too, though – after all, she was still facing danger with Derek. I was going to definitely have to make a deal with Charlotte about that. I was going to have to negotiate with her before we ever got down that aisle, and having Derek either back the fuck off, or, even better, lose his job, would be a part of this negotiation.

I finally made it to Charlotte's house, and my mind filled with dread. I looked down at my hands, and they were shaking. I swallowed hard as I drove up the long drive that led to her mansion. As I sat in front of her house, I took a deep breath. I had to feel calm, because my mind had to be clear. Only with a clear head could I figure a way out of this mess.

As I sat in the car, though, Charlotte came bounding out of the house. She came right up to my car. "Did you tell her?"

"Of course."

She looked at me suspiciously. "How did she take it? And was talking all you did?" She backed off the car a few feet and crossed her arms in front of her. She raised an eyebrow as I just stared at her.

You know that talking is not all we did, bitch. "What do you think?"

She shook her head. "You don't need to tell me, but I can tell you one thing. That won't happen again. Not with you and her. With you and me, that should happen every single day." Then she smiled. "And, believe me, I will be looking forward to that."

I just stared at her, my hands gripping the wheel. My

mind was telling me to run. Run far, run fast, and don't look back. Just go right back to Serena's and whisk her off to my house in Italy, and never, ever, think about Charlotte again.

Of course, we would always be looking over our shoulders. Every minute of every day, we would looking around, wondering when the goons were going to come out and gun us both down.

I couldn't live like that. I couldn't make Serena live like that. So, for now, I had to stay there in that driveway. Staring at that bitch's face. There was nothing else to do, and it made me sick.

Finally, I got out of the car. "Okay, let's go in the house. Let's get our terms straight." I had no leverage at that moment. I knew that. She knew it, too. She held all the cards, because she was the dangerous one of the two of us. She was the one who had the mob ties. She was the one who was desperate and was willing to do anything, absolutely anything, to ensure she got what she wanted.

Still, I was going to negotiate with her as if *I* held all the cards and she had nothing. That was the only way to go into this. If I went into it as if I knew the weak position I had, then she would roll over me. That was the last thing that I wanted, because, well, I wanted to at least ensure that Serena was away from that Derek asshole.

"Come on in," she said, walking into the house. "And let's sit down and try to get this thing done."

I followed her to her terrace, which was set up with a table and chairs and candles as the centerpiece. It looked as if she were anticipating a romantic dinner for two, which is probably what was on her mind. But I was careful to show her, with my body language, that I wasn't having it. None of it. This was a business transaction, nothing more.

I was also going to have to try to negotiate one more

term. One major term – that this marriage was going to be a sham in every sense of the word. I would appear on her arm in public. I would do the dance like a marionette. But I wasn't going to touch her in private. There would be no kissing, no dancing, no sex. We would have separate bedrooms.

That was important. Anything else would be truly betraying my love for Serena, and I wasn't willing to do that. Besides, I doubted that I could get it up for her. I hated her that much.

She was certainly trying, though. I glanced at her as she sat across from me, and I noticed that she was wearing something that was plunging. It was a filmy black number that showed her ample cleavage, and she leaned down so that I could see all of her breasts if I was so inclined. I wasn't, of course, so I immediately averted my eyes.

She continued to lean over the table, though. She was attempting to make it impossible to look down her dress. I was just as determined that I wasn't going to.

"Okay," I said, as she poured both of a glass of wine and snapped her fingers. A waiter came around and laid dinner in front of us. We each appeared to have some kind of a stuffed bird, with some asparagus tips with hollandaise sauce and a side of potato. I shook my head. Charlotte obviously had something in mind, and she was going to try her mightiest to get it. "We need to go over terms."

"Go over terms?" she said, apparently incredulous. "You make this all sound like some sort of business transaction."

"Isn't it?"

"No."

"Well, I think that it is. I need to get this straight with you. This is not about love. It's not even about like. It's about Serena's preservation. And mine, to a lesser extent, but mainly Serena's. Don't ever think differently. The second you start to think that what you and I have is real is the second that I get the hell out of here."

She finally stopped leaning over the table, and leaned back in her chair instead. She was sizing me up, trying to find my weak spot, trying to see if I was bluffing her. "What did you have in mind?" she asked me coolly.

"I would like to dictate the terms of this arrangement. First, there will be no physical contact between us. I will have my bedroom and you will have yours, hopefully in two different wings of the house. Second, you will allow me to fire Derek. After all, I am the managing partner of that firm, so I do have the power to fire him. And, considering what he has done to Serena, I do have cause."

She shook her head. "This isn't what I signed up for. Perhaps I should just put that hit back on Serena and be done. Because you aren't giving me a damned thing here."

"I'm giving you the attention that you crave. Being with me will give you just the right air of danger and intrigue to put you in the spotlight. After all, I'm this notorious billionaire who was accused of murder, and most of the people in this country still think that I might have done it. Once we go public, you'll have the cache that you want. Since I know that you want to become this starlet that is in the public eye at all times, then you'll have that with me." I raised an eyebrow. "Take it or leave it."

"I'm leaving it," she said, perhaps too quickly. "I get what you're saying, and you're absolutely right about that – since you were, by far, the biggest story of this past year, and you continue to draw your share of attention, you definitely will be an asset. But I want more than that. I want you and I to be a real couple. That means a shared bed, and that means sex. You can go ahead and fire Derek. I'm through with him, anyhow. But the other stuff is non-negotiable."

I gave her a high opening offer, and I knew that. I also knew that I had to tread carefully with her. "Okay. Thank you for allowing me to fire Derek. We can sleep in the same bedroom, but not the same bed, and there will be no sex between us. Nothing physical between us."

"Why? You're going to be married to me, so you can just forget about that other woman. You might think that you're betraying her by being with me, but you need to stop thinking that. I'm your future. You and I are the ones who will be together. The sooner you understand that, the better off you'll be."

I narrowed my eyes, trying to figure out how far I could push this. If I threatened to walk away, would she acquiesce, or would she get it in her crazy head that she was going to go nuclear? I realized that I wasn't playing with a woman that had a full deck, and that made her inherently danger-ous. Yet I couldn't possibly give her what she wanted on this. There was no way in hell that I was going to have sex with her. No way in hell that I was going to touch her in any kind of a romantic way. That was simply non-negotiable.

"Those are my terms. You can take them or leave them." That was the same thing that I said before, and I meant it. Of course, inside, I was a mound of jelly. All she had to do was tell me that she wasn't going to play my game, and that she would just go ahead and put a hit on Serena, and I would have done anything that she wanted me to do.

She sighed. "We'll sleep in the same bed. We don't have to have sex, though. That's my final offer."

Grab your copy…
vinci-books.com/wicked-temptations

About the Author

Annie currently lives in San Diego with her two fur-babies, Bella and Toby, and her significant other, Joey. When she's not writing, she's busy reading, cycling all over town, watching cooking shows or classic old movies on TCM (Cary Grant is her favorite) and occasionally watching trashy television shows.